The Road Home

Pete Harrison

Copyright 2021 Pete Harrison

This title is a work of fiction. The names, characters, places and incidents are products of the author's imagination or have been used fictitiously and are not to be construed as real. Any resemblance to persons, living or dead, actual events, locale or organizations is entirely coincidental.

1

Table of Contents

2

Local writer please leave
a review on Amazon

THE ROAD HOME

With Thanks

To

Laura Quirke

NORTH

David watched the sun come up through the grimy window by the side of his bed; he lay on his side and rotated the gold band on his wedding ring finger and wondered if Ruth was doing the same, wherever she may be. The smoke that had permeated the air for months after the end of hostilities had gone now, but the sky was still grey and depressing even though it was the height of summer. David never looked forward to going outside, as the acrid burnt smell still hung around and hit his senses every time.

He peered over the side of his bed and looked at the man sleeping on the bottom bunk.

"Harry, are you awake?"

The figure below rolled on to his back and groaned.

"No, I'm still asleep. Sod off."

"Fat Ali will be here in a minute. I need to know if you're going to come with me."

Harry swung his legs out of bed and sat with his head in his hands.

"God, I don't know, it's so dangerous and it's not much of a plan."

David likewise swung his legs out and leaned forward to bring his friend into view.

"We don't know what's out there so we can't plan. All we are sure of is that there's a strip south of Birmingham that's a demilitarised zone. If we can make it there, we'll be safe."

"Birmingham's a hundred and twenty miles away."

David wanted to convince his friend but he was happy to go it alone if he had to. He was convinced that Ruth, wherever she was, would try to make it home to Stratford upon Avon in the neutral zone, and he wanted to be there when she did.

"We only need to make it out of the camp, they won't come after us. There aren't enough of them here as it is. Lazy bastards will expect their mates to capture us somewhere along the line."

The door of the hut flew open and a very large man loomed in the entrance. He was dressed head to foot in black and wore a black bandana; the obligatory beard reached down to his chest.

"Up, you lazy bleedin' infidels."

He bellowed in a Scouse accent and laughed as he did every morning. 48 men raised themselves from 12 rows of bunk beds each side of the Nissan hut. The menacing figure began to bang on the doorframe with the long bamboo stick he held in his right hand, while his left hand gripped the handle of the short sword that was tucked in his waistband.

"Outside in five minutes, if you know what's good for you."

The men all pulled on trousers and boots and began to button up jackets as they traipsed out of the hut. Once outside they lined up to be marched to the clubhouse that had once been the central point of Mossock Hall Golf Club. Here they were served a breakfast of tea and porridge every morning before being shipped out to the fields in two old coaches.

The men ate in silence. There were only five guards, but they were heavily armed and they had shown early on that they were not afraid to use their weapons. A couple of beheadings had served as a demonstration of the seriousness of the victors' intentions.

David had noticed that when the coaches returned after a day's work, two guards drove them away to park in a separate compound. This left only three guards to keep an eye on the prisoners. Half the men tended to go to the clubhouse, and the others went back to the bunkhouse - so this would be the moment to slip away. And as soon as they reached the tree line, they would be free.

David decided not to mention his plan again to Harry. If he let him mull it over instead of nagging then he just might see it merits.

The day passed without incident. The work in the fields was pretty mundane and didn't require a lot of skill. David pondered whether to enlist the help of some of his fellow prisoners to create a diversion for his escape, but bringing someone else into his confidence would be just one more complication. Better to rely on the men realising what was happening, and hope they would kick up a fuss to help him.

The day began to drag, but as the time approached for them to return to the camp, David began to feel very nervous. When they were dropped outside the clubhouse, David moved to stand next to Harry and watched as the coaches drove off. David gave Harry one more chance - the three guards were out of sight.

"You coming, or what?"

He didn't wait for an answer but began to run for the trees. Within seconds he could hear Harry panting hard behind him. They were about 50 yards short of the trees before they heard a guard shouting. David didn't look back, but as he reached the tree line, he heard shots ring out.

Diving into the undergrowth, he looked round. Harry was sprawled face down on the ground about five yards short of freedom; the back of his head had a gaping, bloody hole in it. Just as David had hoped, the guards weren't pursuing, they were trying to deal with the remaining prisoners who were causing a disturbance.

David scrabbled up and began to run again, fighting his way through scrub and undergrowth.

It was well known that, since the end of the very short war, all the cities and most large towns had become no-go areas. The enormous loss of life from bombings, nuclear and conventional, had left these areas full of rotting bodies that no one was prepared to deal with, instead preferring to keep away from the stench and the rats and flies to let nature take its course. The victors – those who had survived - had re-established themselves in the smaller towns and villages that were untouched by the conflict. Combatants from the losing side were executed without mercy; families of the wrong religion were executed or put into concentration camps to work on the fields. David planned to make his way to Liverpool to get the supplies that he would need before continuing south. He just needed to keep away from any buildings until he got there.

David kept running until he reached the motorway. It may have been less than a mile away, but he began to feel the strain of not eating since breakfast time. As far as he could remember, it was the M58, but these things were not so important now.

His destination was Aintree racecourse. David had decided that it would have been deserted since the war broke out and so there should be nothing of interest there to the victors. He remembered, too, the happy times he and Ruth had spent there at race meetings not so very long ago, and thought that the security of its high boundary fence would offer him a safe haven as long as it remain unbreached.

David followed the motorway towards Liverpool, keeping out of sight as best he could alongside the hard shoulder. There was no traffic whatsoever, but he didn't want to take any risks. At some point he would need to cross the carriageways, and he didn't fancy being caught out in the open.

He continued until he reached a point where a minor road crossed over the motorway. Cautiously, he crossed underneath the flyover, stopping in the middle to take stock and listen for the sound of anything approaching. Nothing.

Once over the motorway he joined the minor road, and eventually he reached the outskirts of Aintree. At first glance, everything looked normal, with houses seemingly untouched by the conflict - but on closer inspection David could see that windows and doors were smashed, brickwork had been pock marked by bullets. Dead bodies of all ages were littering flower beds here and there. There was no discernible life, and an eerie lack of noise; no birds sang, and the smell and sense of death permeated the whole area.

He quickened his pace, and reached another motorway, convinced by now that he was very unlikely to encounter anyone. As it began to get dark, he kept to the shadows, making slow progress, and eventually the stands of the racecourse came into sight. As he had hoped, the external fence was intact, and the complex had not been turned into some sort of military camp. There was no sight or sound of any human life, so he quickly scaled the fence and made a bee line for the betting shop under the main stand.

Knocking out the glass panels from one of the cashier positions was easy. He clambered through and then made his way into the main hall of the stand, where a soft drinks vending machine stood. Smashing the front with a stool, he grabbed first one bottle of water and then another, slaking his thirst.

Before it got too dark David found the stairs and made his way up to the restaurants and the kitchen, in search of something to eat. Unable to find anything that wasn't already rotting, and no tinned food that could be eaten cold, he went in search of another vending machine, and dined on a meal of crisps and chocolate.

After an undisturbed night's sleep on the thick carpet, under a table in the hospitality suite, David left the racecourse and set off in the direction of Bootle.

Things were pretty much the same as the day before - devastation everywhere. But the body count increased, along with the smell of rotting flesh, death and decay. Finding a newsagent, he broke in and was glad to get a little relief from the stench. Once inside he rifled through magazines, until he found information on gun shops. He opted for a local one, 'Aladdin's Cave', which specialised in air guns, thinking there was less chance of it having being looted.

Taking a map, he planned his route and set off for his destination. Leaving by the back door, he thought he caught a movement from the corner of his eye. Then came the distinctive 'click - click', familiar from many an American movie, and David swung round to be confronted by a dishevelled man around his own age.

"Where'd you get a pump action shotgun?"

David knew these had long been illegal in the UK.

"Got it off one of them devils dressed in black, throttled the bastard with an electrical cord. What's it to you?"

"I'm on your side, don't want no trouble."

The man gestured with the end of the shotgun.

"This is my manor. On your way and there'll be no trouble."

David cautiously walked off, occasionally looking back at the solitary figure, not sure what to think.

On route to the gun shop, David found a camping shop where he secured himself a top of the range one man tent, a backpack and some high end waterproof clothing. He took a while to fit himself with a sturdy pair of boots, and loaded a camping stove and spare canister into his newly acquired backpack. Breaking into a display cabinet, he added a camping knife to his kit. Boots the Chemist supplied him with various medications and a first aid kit, and a Tesco Express next door was the donor of several packet soups and noodles.

Feeling better equipped for his journey he headed off for 'Aladdin's Cave' in Everton.

David furtively picked his way along the streets, keen to avoid any more run-ins with gun-toting neighbours. He would walk forwards and then backwards, examining every nook and cranny on both sides of the road. All the shop fronts were smashed, and he was very aware of the crunching of broken glass under his boots.

Progress was slow but David didn't encounter anyone, arriving safely at the gun shop some two hours later. He was not at all surprised to see the shop's window completely gone, the front door hung crazily from its bottom hinge, swinging in the slightest breeze. David shuffled carefully around it, and once inside began to sift through what little stock remained. There were no guns, but he did manage to find a shooting vest which he could wear under his coat and carry ammunition in its many pockets.

Squeezing behind the counter he inspected the heavy steel door to the stock room. As he had hoped, it was badly dented but no one had managed to breach the reinforced structure. Looters had obviously not had time to search for the keys but David set about systematically going through the drawers and cupboards. After a while he found the spare key hidden under a stack of clay pigeon boxes. Gun laws were very strict but that was not going to stop a shop owner hiding a spare key in case he left his own at home.

David ignored the shotguns in racks around the wall, very effective weapons but heavy to carry on a 100 mile journey. He found the top of the range air rifles. These were different from your cheap target pellet guns - they were for serious hunters, and could kill small game at short range.

He had done his research well in the magazine back at the newsagent's, and selected a light weight, high powered, pump-up model along with its accessories and pellets. On his way out of the stock room he noticed some semi automatic air pistols and picked up one of those as well. He locked the door behind him, and hid the keys; no point in making it easy for others.

Cautiously, he stepped back into the street, his new gun slung over his shoulder, and began to make his way out of the city.

Before it began to get dark, he found a house with a shed at the bottom of a large back garden. Breaking into the house, it was apparent from the smell that the house's residents were dead upstairs. But there was bottled water in the kitchen, so David was able to make himself a meal from his packets. He ate it greedily.

Leaving the house to its residents, David followed the garden path down to the shed. His thinking was that anyone searching was unlikely to look there, so he cleared himself a space and bedded down for the night in his new sleeping bag.

Everything was silent outside - but as it began to get pitch black, gunshots could be heard in the distance, and sporadic firing went on through the night. The result of disputes between survivors, maybe? Or the victorious occupying forces hunting down and summarily executing any infidels in their way?

SOUTH

Ruth looked up at the ceiling as the light filtered through the window; she rotated the gold band on her wedding finger, and wondered if David was doing the same. The house would remain quiet for perhaps another half an hour before the old witch would be screaming at her again. The master of the house, a doctor, was pleasant enough, but his wife was going to make sure that Ruth didn't worm her way into his affections. Not that there was any chance of that; she just enjoyed abusing her position; she had power over Ruth.

Ruth considered herself fortunate to be where she was. Thanks to her qualifications, she had escaped the brothels, where most of the women had been sent. She had been a senior nurse before the war, and this doctor had snapped her up as his assistant.

She would savour these last few moments alone and think about David. She was convinced he was still alive, even though she didn't know where he was and hadn't heard from him in four months. She was convinced she would feel it if he were dead. What would he do? He'd make it back to their own home, she was convinced of it, and he would expect her to do the same.

Ruth knew she was somewhere just outside Southampton, but she had no idea how to get to Stratford on Avon. All she knew was that she needed to get there, and the first thing to do was to get away from the people who were her gaolers.

She retrieved the tube of self tan from under her mattress and began to apply some to the back of her hands and her face. She had now used the last of it, but had arranged a new supply from the man in charge of the pharmacy. He knew that she needed it, and had kept it locked away after he found her stealing this last lot. This time she knew she was going to have to offer him sex in return.

It was strange that these religious fanatics could be such hypocrites when it came to pleasures of the flesh. She would offer him what he wanted in return for the cream, but would never deliver as she would be long gone.

Ruth dressed in loose fitting trousers and a black blouse before letting out a long sigh and then putting on the Niqab that covered her head and shoulders and left only her eyes showing. Women workers like herself were required to wear this clothing at all times when interacting with their captors.

Ruth left the house and began the long walk to the hospital. Around 30 minutes into her journey she was as usual passed by the car carrying her boss. And also as usual, he looked straight ahead and ignored her as he was chauffeured to the hospital; he was sitting in his office when Ruth arrived.

"Good morning sir, how are you today?"

Ruth dare not risk anything more familiar; her boss gave an almost inaudible grunt and ignored her. Minutes later he strode out of his office.

"Come, girl."

Ruth followed him as he headed for the wards. As the doctor did his rounds, Ruth took notes; she would update the patients' files as soon as he had finished his tour. The work was mundane but it took up the whole of Ruth's day. She took lunch in a closed room as she had to remove her face scarf. On her return to her office she found the pharmacist waiting for her.

"Here's the stuff you wanted, when will you pay?"

Ruth could smell his body odour; he was so close to her. He clearly didn't wash much, and she had to try hard not to gag.

"Come to the room where I take my lunch tomorrow."

He went to take back the cream, but Ruth snatched it away.

"I'm not going anywhere. See me tomorrow - you won't be sorry."

Luckily the doctor came back to his adjacent office and stared at them sternly through the open door. The pharmacist turned on his heels, and hurriedly left Ruth behind.

Ruth didn't finish work till eight o'clock. The doctor was long gone, and she waited till there was no one else around. She sneaked into the doctor's office and quickly found the drawer where he had hidden half a dozen phials of penicillin, and hid them in her blouse. If she was found with these, with no paperwork or proper explanation, she would be executed on the spot. But she had made a commitment now; she would stay at the doctor's residence overnight and make her escape in the morning.

Later that night, after she had hidden the penicillin and all the other items she was intending to take with her in a pair of adapted bum bags under a loose floorboard in her room, she started to undress for bed. Ruth left her bedroom door open as she took off her clothes. She knew the doctor watched her from a room at the other end of the corridor, and it was a small sacrifice to make to keep the lecherous shit happy. This was definitely, now, more than ever, a man's world.

Infidels were deliberately kept away from any form of information. The Internet was banned now, and been very difficult to access before. Mobile phones and GPS were all disabled by the magnetic pulses from nuclear explosions.

As a prelude to the uprising, terrorists had simultaneously set off devices in big cities all across the country. London, Birmingham and Manchester were completely obliterated, with massive loss of life; other cities were attacked at the same time with conventional explosions.

Total loss of life at the end of hostilities was estimated in excess of 40 million. The British armed forces were completely over-run and the terrorists took command of the skies in aircraft flown in from Eastern Europe. Victory was swift, and the subsequent falling out between the two terrorist factions was almost as swift. Rather than fight amongst themselves, however, they set up a strip across the middle of the country and had half each.

As Ruth played with her wedding ring the next morning, and thought of David, she began to doubt herself. She questioned if she were capable of making the journey. Then she remembered the things that she had hidden under the floorboard. There was no going back.

She rose from her bed and began to dress before the doctor's wife got up. Ruth liked to be out of the house before the lazy bitch had time to chastise her. Everything she was to carry she secreted under her Niqab. She looked a little fatter but not enough to draw any suspicion from anyone who didn't know her well.

She was impatient to get going but waited till her normal leaving time to avoid drawing any attention to herself. After she set off, she kept to her normal pace, so that the doctor in his chauffeured car would pass her at roughly the usual time.

As soon as the car had passed and was out of sight, she turned down the first street she came to and started to walk as fast as she could. She had about 20 minutes' head start and was out of the city before the time she was supposed to be at work.

The clothes that she was forced to wear by her oppressors for religious reasons now afforded her a perfect disguise. She blended in with the other women, all dressed the same, and drew no attention from any other person in the street.

Ruth began to get nervous when she spotted a Nissan pickup truck in the near distance. There was a heavy machine gun mounted on the back, and its black clad operator leaned against it smoking a cigarette. His two colleagues were leaning against the truck having a heated debate in a language foreign to Ruth. They were supposed to be checking the papers of everyone who passed, but Ruth noted that they were too busy arguing. One of the men held his hand out occasionally to check someone at random. Without altering her pace she confidently walked past the men.

"You! Stop!"

Ruth pretended she hadn't heard and kept walking. After several paces, she heard laughter and glanced around to see that the men had accosted one of their friends and were slapping each other on the back. As she progressed out of the built-up area, the number of other people on the road began to decline and she eventually reached a motorway. She looked up and down the empty road, and decided just to go for it - she strode across the carriageway.

Ruth walked all the way to North Baddesley without seeing another person. As she entered the village she proceeded with extreme caution, assuming that she would keep out of trouble as long as she didn't run into anyone. Ruth still had no idea how to get to where she wanted to go. She had never been a great one for geography and like most people had become heavily reliant on sat nav. In the village, road signs gave no clues. Ruth didn't recognise any of the place names and wasn't sure that they would be any help if she did. The

24

biggest sign she came across was for Eastleigh. She decided to head in that direction.

On reaching the outskirts of Eastleigh a little while later, it was clear that the town was a settlement for the victorious army of the south. Ruth realised that she would be walking into trouble, and immediately changed direction. She was increasingly frustrated at her inability to know where to go, having hoped to pick up a map along the way.

She spotted a sign for Winchester, which was at least a name that she recognised, and headed in that direction.

After hours of walking, and becoming increasingly frustrated by her lack of knowledge. Why was she so useless at geography? Why did she know nothing about the positions of the stars, the sun and the moon? Ruth knew that she needed help. But unless she could find a kindred spirit, in the same position as herself, this was going to be impossible.

As exhaustion set in, and with a growing feeling of despair and helplessness, she spotted a house at the end of a long drive. It looked completely isolated. She approached through a wooded area till she could see the back garden of the house, and there she saw six women dressed very much like herself, sitting on the lawn and chatting. Unlike Ruth, however, they didn't have their faces covered. Ruth decided to throw herself on their mercy. She hid the penicillin in the bushes and stepped out onto the lawn. The women looked up. But instead of aggression, she was met with compassion and concern.

"Hello, you okay girl?" asked the woman closest to her.

Ruth began to cry with relief. The other women got up and came over to greet her.

"Come on in, you're safe with us."

Just as Ruth thought her luck seemed to be changing, two men stepped out of the back door, dressed from head to foot in black and carrying AK47 assault rifles.

GOING SOUTH

David had the best night's sleep he had had for a long time. Not being in a room with 47 other blokes was part of it, but the main reason was the quiet outside, just the sound of a gentle breeze, rustling through the trees. It was mid morning before he woke and made his way back into the house where he managed to heat up some more water. Noodles for breakfast didn't seem quite right but it would give him some of the energy he needed for the long walk ahead. He sorted through the cupboards and took everything edible that he could find that wasn't going to weigh him down.

Taking a look upstairs, he avoided the room where the dead bodies were, and checked through the windows front and back for any sign of activity in the street. As on the previous day there was no one about at all, and David was confident that he could make it out into the countryside unobserved.

Half an hour later, packed and ready to go, he ventured into the street, looking and listening for any sign of life. Within an hour he was out of the suburbs and into the countryside.

Avoiding roads as much as possible, David headed generally south, always keeping the motorway, which he had identified as the M6, within sight on his right-hand side. Occasionally, with the lie of the land, he would lose sight of it - and it was on one of these occasions that he came upon an isolated farmhouse, surrounded by woodland.

The woman's agonised screaming could be heard from quite a distance away.

David approached the house with extreme caution. As it came into view, the black flag flying from a pole just above the front door left no doubt as to the identity of its occupants.

The screaming was coming from the other side of the house, interspersed with the sounds of men shouting and laughing. David was about to slip away, quietly, when he heard the woman scream again, and decided he had to take the risk and investigate.

Keeping out of sight he circled deep into the woods until he was on the opposite side of the house. Unslinging his air rifle, he could see what was happening through the powerful telescopic sights.

Two Jihadi guards were in the garden sitting in deckchairs, both with assault rifles laid on the ground beside them and handguns in shoulder holsters. A young woman that David guessed to be in her twenties lay on the ground in front of them. She was on her side, curled up in the foetal position, and David could see that she was completely naked.

It wasn't difficult to work out the cause of her screams, and David began to struggle to contain his anger. His rifle, powerful as it was, would probably not kill a human but would do considerable damage with a well aimed shot from a hundred yards. He lowered himself down, manoeuvred himself into a well camouflaged position, and took careful aim.

The loud crack surprised David as he fired - he had expected it to be silent - and the shot hit the first man just behind the knee cap, penetrating the joint. He fell out of his chair and screamed, writhing in pain on the ground. David kept perfectly still as the second man peered in his general direction, trying to see where the shot had come from. Eventually he gave up and knelt down to attend to his comrade.

David's next shot hit the second man just above the left eye, missing its soft centre by millimetres. It was enough to unbalance the man, who fell over with a bleeding gash on his head. David pumped a second shot into the first man's knee, intensifying his target's screams. He didn't see where his last shot hit the second man - by this time David was on his feet, having dropped the rifle, and was running as fast as he could towards the two men on the ground, his small air pistol in his hand.

As soon he was within range he started to pump shots into both men's right hands before they could reach for their pistols. As they both screamed from the pain, David kicked away the first's pistol. Bending down to pick up the second man's pistol, he could see that neither shot had hit the eyes.

As he looked, a neat hole suddenly appeared in the man's forehead, and David was deafened by a loud bang at his right ear. David looked round to see the naked girl standing there, smoking pistol in hand and a snarling expression on her face. Before he could react, she swivelled on her heels and shot the man with the smashed knee cap twice in the groin. If David had thought his screams before were loud, this was on a different level. He began to worry that someone would hear but when he looked she was striding back to the house holding the gun down by her side.

David could stand the screaming no longer; the air pistol in his hand was not powerful enough to finish the job. He took aim with the man's own pistol and his hands began to shake. He shut his eyes and pulled the trigger, and the screaming immediately stopped. David opened his eyes and threw up.

He went and retrieved his air rifle from the edge of the woods and walked back towards the house. He deliberately avoided looking at the bodies of the two men - he still felt sick and his heart was pounding. Going into the house he began to look for the girl, and found her in a big high back armchair. Her left leg was draped over one chair arm, and her right arm hung over the other, clutching a bottle of scotch by its neck. She was still naked.

"What did you shoot the fucker for? Should have let him suffer."

David didn't know where to look; he tried to focus on the wall just above her head. "He was making so much noise. I had to shut him up."

"I don't see why, nobody bothered about me screaming when they were raping me."

"Well I heard you from quite a distance away. Look, I'm sorry, but can't you put some clothes on?"

The girl took a swig from the bottle, spilling some onto her chest where it trickled down between her bare breasts.

"Not a lot of point really, I think you've seen all there is to see."

She got up and left the room anyway. David sat in the chair she had vacated. When she came back she was dressed in tight leather trousers and a short sleeved t-shirt. David couldn't help wondering why she looked ten times sexier now that she had clothes on.

She held out her hand. "Sorry if I embarrassed you. My name's Alice."

They shook hands.

"David."

"How long have they been… you know?"

"They caught me this morning, decided to have some fun before they turned me in. I'd been walking through most of the night to get as far away as possible when I came upon this house. Front door was open so I decided to get my head down for an hour. I was fast asleep when them two walked in."

David stood up.

"I think we had better get out of here, find somewhere safer. You get your stuff together while I go and hide the bodies."

The task of hiding the two men was not a pleasant one. David dragged the men one at a time by their ankles to the edge of the wood. There was a small ditch that he could roll them into and cover them with dead twigs and leaves.

On his return to the house he noticed the blood trails that he had left across the lawn. There was little to be done about that, just had to hope that nobody arrived before the blood blackened and became less obvious.

When he got to the porch the girl was ready for him. She had on a short coat and a small, full backpack. Alice gave him one of the hand guns that she had brought from the house, and they made their way over to where the assault rifles were still lying next to the chairs . It was going to be quite a weight to carry all the weapons, but perhaps they would be able to find somewhere safe relatively easily. Each of them picked up a rifle and slung it over their shoulder.

"Do you know the area around here?"

"No not really, how about you?"

David shook his head and the two of them set off in the direction that he had originally been travelling. It was more than an hour, walking in silence, before they even came upon another building. They were both getting tired, and the girl stopped and slumped down against a tree.

"Let's just have a 10 minute break."

David followed suit on the other side of the tree.

"You want to tell me about yourself, Alice?"

"Not much to tell really. I was in one of the work camps and I managed to escape. I made it for three days before them bastards found me."

"So where were you heading?"

"I really have no idea; it was just good not to be a prisoner."

"So no plan at all then?"

Alice shook her head. David, on the other side of the tree, couldn't see the gesture, but he took her silence to mean that she hadn't.

"I'm heading for the Midlands, eventually; they say there's a neutral zone there."

They stood up to continue their journey.

"How come they didn't put you in one of their brothels? You're a damned attractive woman."

Alice pretended to curtsy.

"Well thank you kind sir, but I never said they didn't."

They set off in search of somewhere they could stay for a couple of days in relative safety. The house, when they found it, was so perfect that they very nearly walked straight past without noticing. Alice had just happened to see what turned out to be a concealed gateway in a very high hedge.

On investigation, it led to a long, overgrown drive that ran for nearly half a mile before it opened out to reveal a small detached house. Staying in the cover of the drive, they tried to study the layout. There were solar panels on the roof and a small wind turbine on top of an outbuilding roof. David dropped down on to one knee.

"This is just too good to be true, there must be someone here."

Alice knelt alongside him and tried to be more positive.

"Perhaps they were away when the trouble started and we're the first to find it."

"Do you think you can give me cover with the air rifle Alice, while I go and have a look?"

"I'll go, it's your gun, and you know it better than me."

Before he could stop her she was on her feet and heading across the lawn. David checked each window in turn, using the scope, until Alice reached the front door. It was locked.

Pistol in hand, Alice searched around the door frame with her free hand and then checked under the pots that surrounded the doorway as well as the ones under the window. She found nothing, turned to face David, and gave a big theatrical shrug. David stood up and began to walk forward.

"Let's try round the back, there might be something open."

Alice was peering in through the downstairs window.

"It's all dusty inside, doesn't look like anyone's been here for ages."

David walked past her and around the side of the building. By now he also had his pistol in hand, opting for firepower over stealth, and cautiously followed the wall until he again turned the corner to reach the back of the house. Alice joined him at the back door which was also locked.

Just as David was considering the feasibility of kicking in the heavy wooden door, something hit him on the back of the head with force. Instinctively, he put his hand to the point of impact and when he took it away, it was covered in blood. His vision blurred, and he passed out and fell to the floor.

CABINET

"One more fucking 'weapons of mass destruction' joke and there's going to be blood on the carpet."

The room fell silent as all those in the room looked at their immediate neighbour.

"Sorry Prime Minister. Laugh in the face of adversity and all that don't you know?!"

The P.M. wasn't impressed.

"50 million dead and the country gone to hell in a handcart, what's funny in that?"

"Well at least we won't have to deal with Brexit."

The heavy gold pen whistled past the Foreign Secretary's ear, missing him by inches.

In an effort to restore order to the room, the Home Secretary got to her feet.

"Perhaps if I gave my report, Prime Minister?"

The room fell silent as the Prime Minister nodded her approval.

The Home Secretary glanced at the bundle of notes she was holding in her left hand.

"On the 23rd March, a co-ordinated attack by hundreds of terrorist cells belonging to two main factions set off explosive devices in major cities across the United Kingdom. Some of these devices were nuclear bombs; others were of the conventional type. Reports of the use of chemical weapons have not been confirmed, but the use of a nerve agent, to wipe out the whole of London, was highly likely.

"The specific number of casualties is unknown. All serviceable fighter aircraft were destroyed on the ground by groups using rocket propelled grenades or aircraft that we believe were supplied and possibly also flown by the Russians. However, we view this as a civil uprising. In the ensuing war, civilians were murdered en-masse and the army was wiped out, except those that escaped to Scotland. Total casualties are estimated at anything between 20 to 40 million.

"The United Kingdom has subsequently been divided, north and south, by two factions which have emerged from the uprising. The British government and their families were evacuated to Jersey, where we are now. We have tried to contact the terrorist groups but they have indicated that they have no interest in negotiating. The European Union has turned its back on us, from fear of the same thing happening in their countries, opting instead for letting anyone who wants to go to England to do so. The United States have offered their support but as yet have not been specific. Are there any questions?"

"Is the nerve agent likely to spread outside of London? What I mean is, is it carried by the wind?"

The Home Secretary again consulted her notes.

"The boffins think it's a derivative of the one used in Salisbury a few years back; they think it's been modified to become harmless after only a few hours. It would have spread, but not far."

"What about radiation from the nuclear bombs?"

"Once again we think it's minimal, but we have no way of knowing."

"Do we have any resistance still left?"

"There are several groups, most notably the SAS, that have retreated to remote areas. We're giving them all a bit more time to get in touch with us before we try to come up with any sort of plan."

The Prime Minister got to her feet.

"Are there any more questions? Right, well it looks like we're on our bloody own again. We need to find a way to get our country back. I expect your suggestions on my desk by tomorrow morning and we'll meet back here in the afternoon. Thank you very much Gentlemen and Ladies."

GOING NORTH

The day had started normally enough. A larger number than usual hadn't turned up for their shift at the hypermarket, but it was an out of town store so sometimes people could experience trouble getting there.

Later, after it all kicked off, it became obvious that those who hadn't turned up had been warned that something was going to happen even if they didn't know what. The first explosions could easily have been mistaken for the rumbling of thunder in the distance, but when the bombs started to go off in the city five miles away everyone, staff and customers, rushed outside to see what was happening. Then panic set in. Customers ran for their cars along with any staff that had transport and set off for who knows where. As usual, lack of information made things worse. Magnetic pulses from several different sources knocked out radio communication, phones and even engine management systems, rendering most cars unserviceable 15 minutes after the attack started. With the shop and car park emptied, six check-out staff stood in a group by the tills. Everyone else was gone.

"So what do we do now?"

The women looked at each other, and the two youngest started to cry.

"Come on you two, it's not that bad."

The continuing explosions and gunfire in the distance suggested otherwise.

"Well we're stuck here, so I suggest we try and find somewhere to hide until we find out what's happening."

Jean, the shift supervisor, pulled out her mobile and inspected it.

"No service, Wi-Fi or 4g, let's get into the stock room and see if we can't find somewhere safe for now."

The girls followed her, happy that someone was making the decisions.

*   *   *

Bob and Ralph were on their way back to their base in Plymouth after being on leave when it happened. Heading south towards Portsmouth on the M3 they were side by side on their motorbikes doing a steady 70mph when Southampton literally began to explode in front of them. As

Royal Marines they had seen active service in the Gulf and had been on deployment in other parts of the world, but they had never expected to see what was now unfolding.

They pulled onto the hard shoulder to assess the situation, as did most of the drivers on each carriageway. Suddenly two jets flew at low level just above them and Ralph said,

"Looks like the Air Force will sort this out whatever it is".

Just then the planes started to launch ground to air missiles in the direction of RAF Swanwick.

"Perhaps not, what the bloody hell is going on?"

Bob was on his mobile to the docks, and before the magnetic pulse knocked the phone signal out, he managed to hear that whatever was going on was terrorist-related. Car drivers close by attempted to start their cars with no success, but Bob and Ralph managed to kick-start their bikes and sped off towards Southampton. Weaving in and out to avoid disabled cars, they slowed as they neared the outskirts.

"It's too bloody dangerous to go much further without knowing what's going on, Ralph."

Bob gestured to a church over to their left, and they set off in its direction. They parked their bikes just outside the church, on the path running through the graveyard, and dismounted.

Bob gestured towards the church vestibule with his large leather gauntlet.

"Let's see if we can get up the church tower and get a better view of what's going on,"

The two entered the church and looked around for a way up. Through a door at the back of the church they found a staircase and were soon out on the walkway near the top of the church tower.

Southampton stretched out in front of them, large palls of smoke pouring upwards from a dozen locations. Sporadic gunfire could be heard from all over the city, and the whole place looked like hell on earth. Ralph could make out, in the near distance, several heavy machine guns mounted on the back of flat bed trucks, with the black flag of a well known Jihadi group flying above the cabs. Black clad soldiers seemed to be firing indiscriminately at anything that moved.

"I think we had better get the hell out of here."

The wail of a police siren in the distance came to a strangled end as the car exploded.

"I think you're right Ralph."

Heading away from the city, Bob and Ralph came upon an out of town hypermarket. The car park was completely deserted and there didn't appear to be a soul around. They made their way around the back and parked up out of sight of the road to consider their options.

* * *

Earlier that evening, the check-out women had settled themselves in the windowless staff canteen. It was now several hours since the hostilities had started and they were still in the dark as to what was going on. Lots of tea had been drunk and they all seemed a little calmer. Jean addressed the group.

"In the absence of any information, I think we had better stay put. When it gets dark I'll venture out and try and get some idea of what's going on."

Shirley, the youngest, looked frightened.

"What do you think is happening?"

"Well it looks like some sort of attack. I don't really know what happens when wars start, I'm not that old."

There was a sudden noise from the stockroom below, and the girls fell silent, looking at each other with frightened eyes. They huddled together as footsteps could be heard approaching the canteen door. The door creaked as it swung open, to reveal two large men clad in motorcycle leathers.

Ralph and Bob introduced themselves, and several of the women burst into tears from sheer relief. Eager for information, they fired questions at the men who told them what they knew.

"I think we are all better off here for now, perhaps we might get a better idea of what's what later on. Has anyone found a radio?"

Ralph went down into the shop accompanied by Sophie who was to show him where things were. They returned a short while later with a cheap portable radio and some batteries. Ralph tuned it in and quickly found a French radio station.

"Does anyone speak French? No, well that's not much use then."

He continued to turn the dial.

Through the crackles on the airwaves, they managed to catch ' …..across the country in co-ordinated attacks, and the Royal Air Force has been completely destroyed on the ground. The British Army is thought to be organising counter attacks but with communication effectively wiped out, the terrorists seem to have the upper hand. People are advised to stay in their homes and not to resist .... This is a public service broadcast from the BBC.'

Bob clicked off the radio and the room fell into reflective silence. Sophie began to sob.

"Now let's have none of that, Sophie," Jean said sternly. "I think we need to bed down here for the foreseeable future, perhaps things might become clearer. Any of you with partners like me must be thinking about why they haven't come for us. Well, I think the simple answer is that they can't."Sleeping quarters were organised. Inflatable mattresses from the camping department and a pair of camping stoves were put to good use by Ralph, first brewing up some tea and then knocking up a hearty meal for the eight of them. They ate together in the staff canteen, in silence.

Reading books and magazines from the stationary aisle, the hours and eventually the days began to pass. There was no sign of activity in the immediate area, but each day Ralph and Bob would go on foot around the quieter roads in the vicinity, always being careful about the route they took back to the hypermarket to make sure that they weren't seen. Information was still impossible to come by either from the radio or from their field trips.

Ten days after the initial explosions in the city, Mary was on cooking duty for the day. She made her way down the tinned food isle with a shopping basket, concocting the evening's recipe in her head as she selected the ingredients. A rumbling noise from outside caught her attention. She was in the depths of the shop and no one looking in could see her, but she could see out as a large articulated lorry rumbled into the car park. Mary's first instinct was to rush forward to greet the newcomers, but common sense quickly kicked in as the lorry made its way around to the back entrance to the store. Leaving her basket on the floor she ran to the stairway that led up to the staff room. Everyone was there, and as she related what she had seen, the room fell silent, everyone looking to each other for some kind of leadership.

Eventually Bob spoke. "OK, we need to keep quiet; they've probably come to stock up and will find everything they need in the stock room."

Ralph locked the staff room door, and everyone sat on the floor as they listened to the noises of men loading up the lorry with boxes.

An hour or so later, the lorry's engine started. It pulled away, and gradually the noise of the truck in motion faded away into the distance.

The group waited for another half hour, listening carefully for sounds of anyone left behind. Then Ralph and Jean crept stealthily down the stairs into the shop and through to the stockroom. They conducted a thorough search before giving the all-clear, and life went back to what had now become their normality.

After their meal, they sat around the table. Imogen voiced her fears: "Are we safe here or not?"

"There's a lot of stock still left so I'm sure they are gonna be back. We have to be vigilant, but for now they don't know we're here," Jean pointed out.

Shirley and Nadia were whispering together at one end of the table which began to irritate Imogen.

"Come on you two, share it with the group, everyone's entitled to an opinion."

Nadia spoke for them both. "We just want to go home."

Imogen replied a little too loudly: "Well I, for one, am not leaving here till we know what's going on out there – at least we're warm and dry and have plenty to eat. Anyone who leaves is going to be putting us all at risk."

In the days that passed, the team worked on fashioning weapons. They all carried hammers from the DIY section which at the very least could be thrown at an assailant. Handles of garden spades made excellent clubs, and kitchen knives were left around the store where they could be retrieved quickly in an emergency.

No-one strayed too far from the store, and they took it in turns to watch the entrance to the car park from a concealed position in the shop.

Sure enough, exactly a week later the lorry returned and again parked around the back of the stock room. Everyone had retreated to the staff canteen where they were keeping quiet sitting on the floor. After loading, the lorry driver decided to explore.

"Hamza, I'm going to take a look around. Won't be long."
"OK, Mo, but we've gotta be out of here in 15."

Leaving his mate to continue piling boxes of tinned food into the truck, the driver found his way to the drinks aisle and helped himself to a bottle of vodka. Unscrewing the top he took a big swig and let out a satisfied 'ahhh'. Bottle in hand, he found his attention drawn to the bottom of the staircase that led to the canteen.

He pulled himself up the stairs, and there ahead of him was the door. He tried the handle, but it was locked. Why would a staff canteen in an abandoned hypermarket be locked? His curiosity aroused, he barged at the door with his shoulder, bursting into the room to be confronted by the six women.

"What the f......."

Before he could complete the sentence, Bob stepped from behind the door and clubbed him viciously on the back of the head. He fell to the floor, toppling two of the chairs and creating such a noise that it alerted Hamza who went to the bottom of the stairs to investigate.

"You alright Mo?" he called up.

Everyone in the room stayed silent as Hamza slowly climbed the stairs. As the room came into view he could see his comrade sprawled on the floor but not the girls who were now crouched down at the back of the room. He stopped, alarmed and confused.

Ralph stepped out, a silhouette in the doorway, and threw his hammer at the man half way up the steps. It hit him squarely between the eyes, fracturing his skull and knocking him out. Hamza tumbled backwards down the stairs, striking the back of his head as he did so. Sophie managed to stifle a sob and fought back tears. Imogen and Nadia hugged each other, and the rest just stared at the bodies, shocked by the violence that had just unfolded. Ralph broke the silence.

"We've planned for something like this. We need to leave and move on. Everyone try to remember what we discussed and let's get moving."

Bob and Ralph set out to deal with the bodies. Finding an abandoned car, they put the bodies inside and pushed the car into a ditch. It was just like any other of the many crashed vehicles strewn along the road. Then they moved the half loaded truck, parking up in a side street as far into town as they could risk, taking weapons found in the lorry's cab back with them.

As dusk began to fall, a silent group of six women and two men moved out of the hypermarket's car park on foot. Quickly, they left the main road and headed unseen into the countryside. The women were dressed in black, their faces covered by the Niqab. The men were also dressed all in black, complete with balaclava and AK47 assault rifles. To all intents and purposes, they were just a group of female prisoners, guarded by two terrorists.

The group walked well into the night at a steady pace and most of the next day without encountering anyone. Finally they came across a remote property that became their home for a time.

It was another three weeks before Ruth arrived on the scene. Relieved to find people who at least had some idea of where they were going, Ruth readily joined them, and the group became nine.

DAVID

David opened his eyes. He could see light, but everything was blurred; his head hurt like hell and felt like it was full of bees. A silhouette of a woman's head came into his field of vision, and he realised he was lying on his back, indoors. He heard talking that sounded like it was coming from far away. Gradually it formed into recognisable speech, and he could hear Alice's voice.

"Are you okay? Can you hear me?"

David went to shake his head but the pain was excruciating.

"Just lie still for a bit, you had a nasty crack on the head."

David squeezed his eyes tightly shut and tried to block out the light. Eventually he managed to say, in a hushed voice, "What the fucking hell happened?"

"You've been hit on the back of the head by some kind of missile. I've managed to drag you inside the door, and I can't see anyone around."

"How'd we get in?"

"Key was under the mat."

Alice disappeared from view and he could hear her going through the downstairs rooms. He assumed she was making sure that the place was secure. He tried to sit up but the room seemed to be spinning round, and his head started to swim. He slumped back down. Alice returned and stood over him, looking down.

"Whoever it was must be out there somewhere, I think we're pretty safe in here for now."

Half an hour later David was starting to feel better, although his head still hurt like hell. He managed to get to his feet and staggered to a sofa in one of the downstairs rooms. There he resumed a now much more comfortable slump. Alice had checked the whole of the house and confirmed that they were alone and the house was secure.

David positioned himself by a window so he could monitor any activity in the garden. Alice was in the kitchen looking for something to eat.

"Cooker works and everything. It must be the solar panels; we can have a nice hot meal for a change."

She sorted through the kitchen cupboards and found a variety of canned foods and some packets of rice.

"How'd you fancy a curry?"

Just the sound of the question made David's mouth start to water.

"Is there any chicken?"

Alice slammed a can down on the kitchen worktop.

"Just wait there; I'll bring you a fucking menu!"

David had been in so much pain that he had not even considered the stress Alice must have had to cope with.

"Look I'm sorry, I didn't mean to upset you. You're doing brilliantly."

"Don't be so bloody condescending; you'll be wearing your food in a minute."

David decided he would be better off keeping his mouth shut and went back to his lookout duties. He thought he saw movement in the trees at the bottom of the garden but put it down to the wind that was beginning to whip up as the skies darkened before the oncoming rainstorm.

A light drizzle began and soon turned to a steady shower. Then the heavens opened. David got to his feet and shakily made his way to the kitchen. Hoping that Alice had calmed down, he tentatively tried to strike up a conversation.

"It's chucking it down outside."

"Yes I can hear it."

"Strange how it makes you feel so much safer when it's raining outside."

Alice pulled a face at him.

"Yeah, till someone knocks on the door."

David decided it was possibly too soon, and went back and sat down.

The meal was eaten mainly in silence. David had managed to find a bottle of red wine - Alice had drunk most of it before they even sat down. The conversation was a little strained and Alice kept resorting to sarcasm, so David tried to be polite and uncontroversial. As soon as it got dark they both went to bed, each in one of the four bedrooms upstairs.

When he woke David could hear that Alice was having a shower, and he was relieved to hear that her mood had lightened - she was singing at the top of her voice. She waved to him as she walked naked past his open bedroom door, drying her hair with a towel as she sang.

David dived into the bathroom as soon as she had gone, and was just starting to wash his hair in the shower when Alice walked in unannounced, and sat on the toilet before engaging him in conversation. He had to hide his embarrassment.

"I think we should stay here for a few days, it seems pretty safe, all things considered."

David tried to keep his back to her and spoke over his shoulder.

"What about what happened when we first arrived, there's still no explanation for that."

"We can have a scout around the area, see if there's any sign of anyone about."

Later as they stepped out of the back door, Alice crouched down and picked up a large marble; it was covered in blood.

"This must be what knocked you out yesterday, probably thrown or fired from a catapult."

"Yeah, but why just do that and disappear?"

"Perhaps they didn't know we were going to get in the house and were just trying to scare us away."

A search of the garden revealed nothing, Alice was all for searching the woods but David wanted to err on the side of caution.

They returned to the house and collected hand guns, locking the house behind them. Alice stood on the perimeter of the wood as David ventured in, keeping her in sight at all times.

It wasn't long before he noticed smoke rising from somewhere deep in the woods. He approached stealthily, and saw it was a camp fire in a clearing that had all but burnt out. The makers of the fire were nowhere to be seen but it looked like there had been a number of people around the fire in the night.

It was deep enough into the woods that they wouldn't have seen it from the house. David began to get nervous and opted to get back to Alice and out of the woods as quickly as possible. In his hurry to get out, he burst back into the garden so suddenly that Alice swung around aiming her gun and almost shooting him.

"Jesus Christ, what the hell are you doing? I could have shot you!"

David was still near to panic; it was infectious, and the two of them broke into a run towards the house, letting themselves in and locking the door behind them. Alice threw herself on the sofa, and David furtively checked through the windows.

"There's definitely been someone out there, probably all night."

Alice was breathing heavily, flushed by the excitement.

"God that was a rush, do you want to have sex?"

"Jesus Alice, what's wrong with you, there's people out there!"

"Yeah I know, but I nearly shot you, I'm so turned on!"

"You can't be serious?"

Alice looked hurt.

"Of course I'm serious, do you want to fuck or what?"

David alternated between checking through the window and looking back at Alice.

"I'm a married man Alice, faithful to my wife."

"I'm not after a relationship – and anyway she's probably dead. I'm just talking about some physical release."

It was David's turn to look hurt.

"Alice you're an incredibly attractive woman, but while there's any chance of my wife being alive it's unfair to go around shagging for fun."

Alice left the room and David didn't see her for the rest of the morning. She was in her room with the door shut doing God knows what. Around lunch time he heard her showering in the bathroom and she came down dressed in a fresh tee shirt and jeans.

"Found these in the wardrobe upstairs, the lady of the house must have been the same size as me."

Even David could see by the way the tee shirt stretched across her ample chest that the lady of the house must have been at least one size smaller.

"I don't think we should stay here too long, there's definitely someone out there. It's only a matter of time until they get up the nerve to come looking."

The afternoon was dull and overcast. A drizzle of the sort that makes your clothes wet through when it doesn't look like it's raining at all made the grey mist look even worse.

Alice wanted to get some fresh food from the vegetable patch at the side of the house. Leaving the door open to give them a quick route to safety if needed, David stood guard with an AK47. He watched the perimeter of the garden while Alice harvested what she wanted, collecting it in a plastic bowl brought from the kitchen. The whole thing passed without incident but both were glad to get back inside the house with the doors locked.

The washed veg was left to drain in the fridge. Alice settled herself on the sofa with a bottle of red wine, and David stationed himself at one of the upstairs windows with the high powered air rifle and scope. He scoured the border where the garden met the woods through a small gap in the sash windows. The eye strain was tiring, and he was almost asleep when he suddenly detected movement. He shook his head to try and clear it, and peered through the magnifying scope.

A pair of eyes swam into view through the green leaves of the undergrowth. David struggled with his conscience momentarily, and decided that anything lurking out there was fair game. Gently squeezing the trigger, he was again surprised by the loud sound that the gun made.

The eyes dropped away and David strained to identify his target but could see nothing. Another few minutes spent surveying the tree line revealed no movement at all. Making his mind up, he decided to go out and find out who he had shot.

David left the rifle at the window and made his way downstairs after picking up his hand gun. Alice was fast asleep on the sofa, the bottle empty. He decided not to disturb her as he made his way through the door.

Walking across the garden, the incessant drizzle deadened any noise. He walked slowly, and the wind rustling through the trees made the hairs on the back of his neck stand on end. As he approached the point where his prey had dropped, he felt tightness in his chest and his breathing became laboured. A rustling to his left was almost enough to make him turn and run for home, but he steeled himself and sank down to his knees at the tree line. David parted the branches to reveal a full grown muntjac deer, shot stone dead through its left eye. He heaved a sigh of relief and made his way back to the house – walking at a slightly faster pace than he would have if he thought Alice had been watching him.

The rest of the afternoon passed without incident. David prepared the evening meal before Alice woke from her alcohol-induced sleep. They shared another bottle of wine with the meal, and the conversation was a lot more amiable than it had been the night before. David related his kill to Alice and they decided that they would recover it in the morning and have some fresh meat.

David was sprawled on his bed when there was a gentle knock on his door. "David?"

"Yeah?"

The door slowly swung open and Alice walked in wearing a big white fluffy dressing gown. She stood at the end of the bed and slowly undid the belt. Holding the two sides, she opened the dressing gown wide to reveal her naked body underneath.

"You sure you don't want some of this?"

RUTH

Ruth immediately liked her new companions. Considering the present circumstances, they appeared to be quite a happy bunch. The two men were the type that you could rely on in a tight squeeze, and all struck Ruth as genuine – what you saw was what you got.

That first evening they made Ruth very welcome. The younger girls especially seemed relieved to have someone new to share their tribulations with.

Jean (the natural but unofficial leader of the girls, having been the most senior in the team back at the shop) was in her late 40s, recently divorced. She had been very happy with life until the start of the present troubles.

She considered herself to be level-headed, and, for her own peace of mind, she managed to get Ruth alone and questioned her at some length. Satisfying herself that Ruth had no hidden agenda, she, too, welcomed Ruth into the group.

They took to each other very early on. Ruth had told Jean about her life under the new regime, and Jean was curious to know why Ruth was so desperate to get away from a relatively cushy number.

"So how come you're here? Where are you heading and why were you so keen to get away?"

"My husband, David, was working up north when all this happened. I'm sure if he can get away he'll head back to the neutral zone. It's where we used to live, just outside Stratford upon Avon. He'll expect me to be there."

Bob overheard this as he entered the room.

"Well it's as good an idea as anything else; we might as well all try to get there."

Jean nodded her agreement.

"It's good to have a plan; we can stop here tonight and head for the Midlands in the morning."

*   *   *

Syed and Sonny were lifelong friends. They were born in the same street in Bradford within days of each other, they went to the same schools, and when they were older both studied at Bradford University. Their fathers were leading lights at the mosque which the boys attended without fail.

Plans were well advanced for Sonny to marry one of Syed's sisters. Shortly before the trouble started both boys - although concerned about the developing terrorist situation - would in no way have considered themselves to be radicalised. They loved their way of life, but they had heard the rumours around the mosque and had realised that they may have no choice. After the war broke out they swiftly had to make a decision as to whose side they would be on. It was easier to go along with the radicals who were gaining support at a tremendous rate. The alternative - making a stand against them - would swiftly lead to their own deaths.

The hostilities changed their lives dramatically at a stroke. They felt no animosity to any other group or religion, but now found themselves miles away from home in the south of England. The two of them were manning a heavy machine gun on the back of a flat bed truck. They were guarding a crossroads, both dressed head to foot in black, including balaclavas.

As they prepared to hand over to two comrades who had just arrived, Syed spotted a small wisp of black smoke above the trees about a mile away. Syed suggested that they go and investigate, but Sonny wasn't keen.

"Let's just go back to the camp mate, it's probably nothing anyway."

Syed, however, had other ideas.

"Come on, it's been a boring day and it'll be a boring night as well. Let's go and take a look."

*   *   *

Ruth's party had stopped for the night in a clearing in the woods, and Mary was boiling up some water on one of the small camping stoves. Ralph had asked her several times before not to do this until darkness fell but she was keen to get a hot drink and chose to ignore him.

A small puff of wind blew dried leaves onto the flame, and started a small fire. Quickly, the girls stamped it out, but not before a cloud of black smoke had drifted up into the sky – and attracted the attention of Syed and Sonny.

Syed and Sonny's noisy approach gave the party time to prepare. When they burst into the clearing, the girls were seated on the floor wearing full head coverings. Ralph was standing guard over them.

Sonny addressed Ralph. "What's happening here, why are you out in these woods?"

"We're moving them north; we seem to be a little lost."

Syed was suspicious. "Yeah, but where are you supposed to be going?"

An incredibly nervous Sophie spoke up without thinking.

"Who are they? Why are they questioning us?"

Syed starred at Ralph inquisitively wondering why he hadn't slapped the prisoner down, a woman prisoner at that, interrupting a conversation between two men.

Ralph felt the situation slipping away from him and tried to cover it by saying just a little bit too loudly: "Andover! We're going to Andover!"

Syed was even more fidgety now, and just as he began to unsling his AK47, Bob stepped out from the tree line and hit him just behind the ear with the butt of his weapon. Syed dropped to the floor stone dead. Sonny stared down at his dead best friend, then began to howl.

Bob kicked Sonny with the heavy heel of his boot, cracking Sonny's knee cap. Ralph put his hand over Sonny's mouth and dragged him down to the floor where he pushed the hysterical man's face into the soft ground. When he had stopped struggling, Bob and Ralph turned the quivering wreck that Sonny had become over, sat him up, bound his hands and put a gag in his mouth.

The group stood in a circle around Sonny discussing the situation.

"We have to kill him, we have no choice."

Several of the women nodded in agreement and Bob began to reach for his knife. Sonny stared at him with terrified eyes; Jean stepped between the two men.

"Wait! We can't just kill a prisoner, that's murder!"

"Well what do you suggest, he'll get us all killed."

Mary crouched down in front of the prisoner, pulled down the gag, and asked gently: "What's your name?"

"Sonny, I'm called Sonny, I'm one of you really. I'm British."

Mary tried to calm him. "Where's your base? Where were you going back to?"

"Our headquarters is about five miles away from here."

Mary pulled the gag back into his mouth and stood up. The group moved away leaving Bob guarding the young man.

"Look, he's not going to be able to move very quickly with that smashed knee. We can't just kill him, it's barbaric. I say leave him tied up here. We can be miles away before he finds any help."

Ralph reluctantly agreed. "Okay, if that's the way you want it. But I think we're making a big mistake."

The group made immediate preparations to move out, and after checking that Sonny was securely bound, they melted away into the woods.

SNIPE

Trooper 'Tommo' Reynolds covered up his L115A3 AWM and reluctantly left it in position. It was fixed and sighted in a small hollow on top of a hill. He had become understandably attached to his sniper rifle in the last few months and found it comforting to have nearby. He knew it was nearly impossible for anyone else to find, even by accident, but took a reassuring look back when he was less than a hundred yards away.

Tommo silently made his way along the tree line until he was three quarters of a mile from his original position. After checking both ways he stepped out onto the verge of a dual carriageway and stopped and listened for any sound. Moving to the nearest tree he quickly attached a small piece of green cloth to an overhanging branch. Hastily he stepped back into the trees and then stealthily made his way back to his firing position. After a pee and a final look around Tommo crept into the hollow alongside his rifle and pulled the camouflage netting over himself and his gear. He checked his watch and settled down to sleep for the next four hours.

Trooper Reynolds woke but kept his eyes shut whilst he listened intently to the sporadic traffic passing on the road below. He checked his watch and decided to act in around 30 minutes, just before the light began to fade.

With slow, deliberate movements, Tommo manoeuvred himself into his firing position, and silently eased a round into the chamber with the bolt action. Only then did he pull the butt of the rifle into his shoulder before flipping open the rear cover of the scope. He easily located the small piece of cloth, and as there was very little wind, he knew he needn't make any last minute adjustments. He waited and listened for the next vehicle to come towards him along the road.

Tommo dismissed the first truck as it was a petrol tanker, and any resultant explosion and fire would make it impossible for him to leave the area till daybreak. The second was ideal, a canvas-covered eighteen tonner probably containing ordinance or supplies. There was a co-driver and the possibility of troops in the back. As the driver's face appeared in the crosshairs of his scope, he gently squeezed the trigger and absorbed the kick back in his shoulder.

Tommo had great faith in his own ability. Without bothering to look at the result of his work, he rolled onto his back and tipped the rifle from its stand onto its side, ensuring both he and his rifle were completely hidden.

Nearly a mile from his firing position the bullet smashed through the windscreen entering the driver's head just above his left eye, and blew off the back of his head. His involuntary reaction was to slam his foot down on the accelerator. The co-driver lunged for the steering wheel, an action that would prove fatal as he pulled it towards himself too forcibly. The truck lurched to the left, the nearside wheels ploughed onto the verge, and finally the truck rolled onto its side. As the windscreen shattered, the co-driver was thrown through it into the road. The two men in the back were crushed under the heavy packing cases full of food supplies. Some spilled onto the highway.

Tommo listened to the cacophony of sound that began to reach him but resisted the temptation to look. Only when there was complete darkness would he vacate his firing position and move completely away from the area along the path that he had scouted the day before.

ALICE

David had his eyes tight shut. He instinctively knew that the person clearing their throat wasn't Alice; she was making altogether different noises. He opened his eyes to see the large black man standing at the end of the bed, with two women at his side. Alice continued to ride David, deep into her own pleasure and oblivious to anything else that was going on. The intruder just raised his eyebrows and waited for her to finish. David was rapidly losing interest and Alice stopped and stared down at him.

"Don't fail me now big boy, I'm almost there."

A large smile spread over the black man's face.

"Don't be too hard on him, babe."

In a split second Alice was off David and off the bed, she snatched the pistol from the bedside table and had it pointed at the unwelcome visitors. She made no attempt to hide her nakedness.

David, however, tried to hide his rapidly diminishing manhood with his hands.

"Any geezer would have trouble performing with us as an audience."

The black man was flanked by two teenage white girls who were giggling behind their hands. His movements were slow and deliberate, designed so that Alice wouldn't do anything rash. He turned to leave.

"We'll wait for you downstairs if you want to put some clothes on and join us."

Moments later David and Alice joined them. As well as the three they had encountered in the bedroom, there were also two boys aged about twelve. Alice threw herself into an armchair in her youthful way, but David stayed in the doorway. The first young boy half smiled at him but the second just glared, his eyes full of hate. The large black man stood up to greet them.

"You'll have to excuse Ben, he hates everyone at the moment. Rebels killed both his parents. I'm afraid it was Ben who introduced us with his sling shot when you arrived."

David instinctively touched the back of his head.

"Well he's a bloody good shot; you'd have to give him that."

"My name's Winston. These two lads were my pupils at school before the troubles. We were out on a field trip when everything started, and so far we've managed to evade capture."

Alice eyed the two girls up and down.

"What about these two delightful young ladies, where did you find them?"

"We can talk for ourselves, he's not our dad."

"Well I'd sort of guessed that, where you from?"

"We were doing a shift in McDonald's when the bombing started. When we got home our house was gone. We joined up with these three a couple of months back."

David spoke to the other girl. "So are you two sisters then?"

"Yeah, she's the oldest."

Alice pulled herself out of the chair.

"Well, I best get started then if we're going to eat."

Alice and the girls moved to the kitchen where they began to prepare a meal. The luxury of an electric cooker powered by the solar panels on the roof was a great asset. They managed to recover the muntjac from the garden, and Alice crudely butchered it, discarding all but the best cuts.

A stew was knocked up in the largest pan that they could find. Root vegetables from the garden were sautéed and added to the pan, and the resulting dish smelled delicious.

David prepared the table for the seven of them, and Alice brought over the big pot. After everyone was served, she popped back to the kitchen and returned with another bottle of wine. David gave her a disapproving look, but she just stuck out her tongue.

Winston related their story as everyone enjoyed their meal. He had been a geography teacher in a northern secondary school, and had taken a minivan full of pupils to a farm for a field trip. They had left the school early in the morning and had almost arrived at the farm when the bombing started. Unsure what to do, Winston had immediately headed back to the school only to find the place in chaos. He immediately set about returning his charges to their homes, and had delivered everyone apart from Ben and Steve. When they arrived at Ben's house it was badly damaged and on fire, and Ben's parents were dead in the front garden.

Winston drove the van as quickly as possible out of town and into the country. Steve was obviously distressed – he had no idea what had become of his own parents - but Winston managed to convince him that they were still alive, and that

Steve would be reunited with them after the troubles were over.

Winston had plenty of experience of living off the land, having travelled extensively as a young man. He knew the importance of keeping away from the enemy until they could establish a place of safety. It was pretty easy to avoid detection, as the enemy seemed to have little interest in looking for anyone.

The girls' house, an end of terrace, had been completely demolished by random shelling from outside of town. Confused about what was going on, like most people at that time, the two of them hid in the first vacant house they came to. There they witnessed the abuse and murder of a family that were dragged from their home. Quickly they became convinced that they were not safe and headed for the relative protection of the countryside.

They survived by spending time in farm buildings where the owners had been 'cleansed'. Groups of militia travelled round in flat bed trucks rounding up people of working age and dispatching any that they thought wouldn't be useful.

The farms that were safe for the girls were obvious as no attempt was made to bury the dead. The two groups met up in the countryside a few miles away from where they were now.

They had discovered the house a matter of hours before the arrival of Alice and David, and had been observing the place for any signs of life when David had appeared at the back door. In his temper, Ben had launched his catapult attack on David unexpectedly, and Winston had decided they should retreat back into the woods until they could work out whether Alice and David were friends or foe. It had been ridiculously easy to get into the house undetected but considering what they found Alice and David doing, it wasn't surprising they weren't heard. Winston began to clear away the dirty dishes from the table.

"Well thank you for that lovely meal. I know you don't know us, and you probably feel safer on your own, but would it be okay if me and the kids stay here for a couple of days?"

David looked to Alice, who shrugged her shoulders. David took this to mean the decision was up to him.

"This is an ideal place to hole up in for a few days. I don't think we have any objection to you taking advantage of it."

THE FARM

Ruth's group deliberately headed out from the clearing in the wrong direction, to confuse anyone that Sonny might eventually send after them. Travelling swiftly, they changed direction twice in order to conceal their trail, eventually setting out in the direction that they needed to go.

All day and on through the night they walked, avoiding populated areas, and taking short breaks as infrequently as possible. Four hours of the following afternoon was spent sleeping deep in the woods, well away from any roads or human habitation.

The rain had stopped while they slept, but when they began to move again the depressing drizzle restarted. It was early evening, but the gloom made it hard to see where they were going - and as the dampness began to penetrate their clothing, Ralph began to sense that one or two of them were on the verge of giving up.

They were trudging up a minor road close to some small villages when Ralph called a halt at the end of a long tree-lined drive. A house and some farm buildings were just visible in the distance. He looked up at a wooden sign hanging from a pole and creaking in the wind. He could just make out 'Barn Owl Stables' carved into the wood.

"Let's have a look down here and see if we can find somewhere warm to shelter through the night."

The whole party as one wordlessly turned and began to walk up the drive. About halfway up Bob, who was leading, signalled for everyone to stop.

"Get behind these trees so that you can't be seen from the road. Me and Ralph will go the rest of the way and check out the lie of the land."

He handed Ruth one of the assault rifles taken from Sonny and Syed.

"Only use it if you have to."

Ruth reluctantly took it. "I've never fired one of these."

"But you have fired a gun before?"

"Yes, but only a shot gun."

Bob just smiled and winked at her.

"Well, you know which end the bullets come out, that's half the battle. The safety is off so just be careful."

Bob and Ralph left the women behind and continued on towards the farmhouse. As they got closer, they picked up a putrid smell, the smell of death.

Moving into the gap between the farmhouse and the stables, the smell grew intense. A door bereft of its glass panels swung back and forth in the wind, occasionally cracking into the door frame. The thump, thump, thump sound in the dreary wet night caused the hairs on the back of their necks to stand on end.

As he rounded a corner, Bob could see paddocks, each with at least one horse. The horses had been left out when the troubles started. One or two had eaten the grass down to bare earth and they were all undernourished, but not badly.

The two men moved towards the farmhouse. Ralph held the door whilst Bob crunched through the broken glass and entered the house.

He knew immediately that the building had been unoccupied for some time. There were signs that someone had been through the house in a hurry, looking for food or gathering belongings for a quick exit. Bob stayed by the front door as Ralph searched inside.

Eventually Ralph gave the all-clear, and both men relaxed. Ralph put his gun onto the kitchen table and deposited himself into the battered rocking chair. Bob checked through the kitchen cupboards.

"We should be alright for the night here if we don't show any light."

"Yeah, we're far enough away from the road I think."

Bob started to pull some tins from the cupboards.

"It's a pity we can't organise a hot meal though, I think we all need one."

Ralph got up and headed back to where they had left the rest of the party, and Bob decided to check out the source of the smell. He left the farmhouse and walked over to the stables.

He could see in the gloom that most of the stables were empty – but sadly one of the horses had been left shut in, without water, and had eventually starved to death. Its rotting body was the source of the smell. When he returned to the house the whole party was there.

"I suggest that we all get some sleep now. Ralph and I will do a couple of hours each on lookout if two of you ladies will take over in the early hours of the morning."

The women all gratefully agreed and went to get some sleep.

Ruth woke early and managed to creep out of the bedroom without disturbing anyone. Going downstairs she found Bob sitting in the kitchen keeping a lookout through the window.

"Morning, where's Ralph?"

"He's gone down to look at the horses."

Ruth started to go outside.

"Don't go too far away, we still don't know what's out there."

She walked down the gravel track towards the paddocks and found Ralph leaning on the wooden fence looking at the horses.

"You'd never believe there was a war on," he said.

Ruth shook her head. "I don't think there is. I think we lost."

"What was it all about? Bloody religion again I suppose."

Ruth leant on the fence next to him, stared out across the countryside and offered an observation.

"Still it's good to be alive."

Ralph put his hand on hers and she quickly jerked it away, turned round and leant her back on the fence. "I hope my David made it."

Ralph began to open the gates to the paddocks.

"We might as well let them roam free; none of this was their fault."

As they walked back to the house, Ruth began to guide him to the farm buildings.

"The cooker's gas, bottled gas, its run out - but there's bound to be some in the equipment store."

An hour later they all sat down to a hot meal that Bob had cobbled together, corned beef and bean stew with boiled potatoes. That would have been a strange thing to have for breakfast six months ago, but in present circumstances it was very welcome. The girls cleared up the breakfast things as Ralph and Bob remained at the kitchen table.

Ralph addressed the group. "Any of you girls ride?"

A couple looked at him a bit puzzled. Sophie giggled.

"Horses! I mean do you ride or have you ever ridden horses?!"

Ruth put down the dish and the cloth she was drying it with and turned to face the men.

"I had my own hunter in Stratford before the troubles. He was turned out so hopefully he will be alright."

She looked at the other girls who all shook their heads. Bob got up from his chair and spoke with his best John Wayne voice.

"Well, Ralph, you know I don't ride so you must be looking for a new pardner!"

Ralph smiled. "I was thinking we could stay here for a few days but we're going to need supplies." Pointing to the road just visible in the distance through the window, he added "I was thinking of riding to the nearest village to see what we can find.

"There's been no traffic along there while we've been here, but the safest option is to go across the fields till we find something. We can carry a lot if we go on horseback."

Imogen and Nadia took a quick look around the farm buildings and located what might be the tack room - a shipping container that was heavily padlocked. Not wanting to make a noise by forcing off the lock, everyone joined in the search of the farmhouse for a key. A likely looking candidate was found. Ralph and Ruth went down to the paddocks to select a couple of horses. When they returned, the tack room was open and they found a couple of saddles that matched their horses.

Later that afternoon Ralph and Ruth were waved off by the rest of the group as they set off across the fields. Each rode a hunter and had an AK 47 slung across their backs. Ralph also led a large pony on a lead rope which they would use to carry their spoils on the return trip.

They travelled in silence, almost mesmerised by the scenery in front of them. It was the perfect English summer afternoon, and made it easy to forget the recent conflict.

The top of a Church steeple came into sight, towering over a small copse in the distance.

"We'll head for that church Ruth and hope that it's a small village. We can leave the horses in the woods and go in on foot."

The wood was large enough and dense enough for the horses to be well hidden. They tied them up in a small clearing with plenty of grass, and unslung their automatic rifles before cautiously moving forward.

Emerging from the wood, they found just the type of place that they were looking for: a small village, the sort with one pub and one shop, and a minor road running through it. It was eerily silent, as they had expected, and they moved forwards keeping close to the walls of the buildings.

Apart from several abandoned cars, there was no indication that any traffic or people had been through recently.

Ruth crossed the road towards a large, wooden building painted dark green, with a sign over the door: 'Flyfield Village Hall'. She tried to peer through the window but couldn't see past the dirty curtains inside. Meanwhile Ralph had reached the door. He pulled it open and carefully stepped inside. He was quickly back out before Ruth had reached him.

"Don't go in there."

He turned to the side and was violently sick; Ruth had her hand on the door handle.

"Don't go in Ruth, you don't need to see that."

He was vomiting again before he had finished the warning.

Ruth pulled open the door and walked in undeterred, even after the smell had hit. She stopped dead at the sight before her.

Hanging from the rafters were around 40 men, women and children. Nooses had been put around their necks, and they had been hauled six feet above the ground.

Ruth stood looking up at them, tears streaming down her face. Ralph grabbed her by the elbow and pulled her back outside.

"Why the children?" she sobbed. "Why do that to any of them, but really - why the children?"

Ralph just looked at her. His expression said it all - there are no answers, no words for the horror they were witnessing.

Shuffling, dejected, they made their way up the street, Ruth following behind Ralph, her tears still flowing.

"Anyone still in the village must have been rounded up and taken in there. The kids would have been terrified."

They found the village shop. It was locked up.

"Best if we break in around the back, so it looks like it's untouched," suggested Ralph. Ruth nodded her agreement, and they found their way to the back entrance.

It was very dark in the back of the shop, and they didn't want to risk drawing attention to themselves by using a torch, so checking out the stock was a painstaking affair.

"Just go for packet stuff, Ruth, it's lighter to carry. Pasta would be ideal - it keeps forever, and the sauces to go with it."

Ruth attempted to lighten the mood. "You sure you wouldn't like to prepare your own sauces?" she asked, jokingly.

"We can take a couple of bags of cans of pasta sauce," Ralph replied, completely missing the sarcasm.

They began to pile stuff into large cloth 'bags for life' that they had found behind the shop counter. Half an hour later, they had eight large bags piled ready to go by the back door.

Ralph stared down at the bags with his hand on his hips.

"We're going to have to make a couple of trips. I'll carry the bags and you cover us with the AK."

"I can carry bags as well; I'm not some weak female, you know."

"I wasn't suggesting that for a minute, Ruth. But we would be no good with rifles slung over our backs if we were attacked, we'd be dead before we could unsling them."

Realising her mistake, Ruth agreed. They set off back to the woods, Ralph carrying four large bags of provisions and Ruth five yards behind with her AK 47 at the ready. Crossing over the road, they retraced their steps past the village hall. Both purposely looked away.

Just as they reached the edge of the village, Ralph, some way ahead of Ruth, turned a corner to be confronted by a very large Rottweiler sitting in his path. Ralph stopped as the dog began to growl and bare its teeth, saliva dripping from its jowls. Ralph dropped the bags and the growling stopped as the beast licked its lips. Ruth was still to turn the corner when she heard a strange man's voice.

"What do we have here then?"

Stepping out of a doorway close behind the dog was a very tall man, over 6 foot 4 wearing a long black coat and carrying an old double barrel shot gun aimed directly at Ralph's chest.

"Where did you get that stuff from then, old boy?"

Ralph realised that he had no chance of unslinging his gun which he had deliberately worn diagonally across his back to stop it slipping off his shoulder.

"The little shop around the corner."

"I guess you saved me a trip then," he sneered.

Ruth suddenly appeared around the corner, the assault rifle to her shoulder.

"Drop it," she barked.

"And what if I don't?"

"I can shoot you and the dog with one burst from this thing, if that's what you want."

The stranger hesitated, then slowly lowered his weapon.

"Tyson, lie down."

The dog did as he was told.

Ruth relaxed and lowered her weapon, but just as she did so, a large man launched himself through an open doorway to her left, throwing his full body weight on her left shoulder. She went down like a sack of spuds with the man on top pinning her to the floor. Her weapon skidded across the floor. Ralph lunged forward but the dog grabbed him by the leg of his trousers. The man with the shotgun took control.

"Okay everyone, calm down."

The new arrival got to his feet and retrieved Ruth's gun leaving Ruth lying on the ground gasping for breath.

"Leave him, Tyson."

The dog obediently let go. The man gestured to Ruth with the barrel of the shotgun.

"Up you get, darling, you need to help your man carry these bags."

The uneasy party left in the direction that Ralph and Ruth had been travelling. The dog was leading, followed by the two new prisoners carrying the bags of supplies. Following on, but a little way back, were the two men with guns.

"Don't suppose you two want to tell us where your camp is?"

The question was ignored by Ralph and Ruth.

"We'd better go back to our place, in that case."

TOMMO

Trooper Reynolds had watched with interest as the couple entered the village. He had spotted them way in the distance when they came across the fields on horseback. He had left his position to relieve himself before settling down to wait for dusk, when he planned to find his next target.

Tommo returned to his sniper rifle. It had occurred to him that the pair might cause some disturbance that could compromise his attack on vehicles. But his planned attack was a few hours away and he could easily abort. Nevertheless his curiosity was such that he decided to keep an eye on them for the time being.

With his ranging binoculars, he was able to track the couple as they entered the village. He was a little surprised at their lack of precautions as they walked through the streets. The man's reaction on exiting the village hall told Tommo that something monstrous had happened inside, something he himself would never go looking for. He found it less than useful to have any emotional feelings about his enemies.

The girl had shown no physical signs of distress when she came out; she was obviously made of stern stuff. Tommo silently approved the couple's decision to enter the shop around the back; while they were inside, he took it upon himself to scan the area around.

The two men and the dog were not as easy to spot. They passed between the shop and the house next door, unseen by the two rifling through the shop's contents, and slipped quietly across the road, turning into the next side street where they waited out of sight.

As the couple came out of the shop carrying provisions, Tommo's first thought was to fire a shot to warn them of the danger - but decided against it. He couldn't be sure that the two groups would be hostile towards each other - and, if the woman stayed back, they should have the upper hand in spite of the dog.

As the drama unfolded, Tommo let out an audible groan when the girl lowered her weapon and got mullered by the man hiding to her left. Satisfied that there was not going to be any bloodshed in the village, he decided to leave them to their fate and he would take a nap while waiting for his next target to arrive.

OLD MAN

Things in the house began to settle into a routine. Winston seemed happy that his group had found a place of refuge, and the two young girls were happy that they had somewhere stable. In their eyes, Winston could do no wrong. Whatever he decided was always going to be all right with them.

The two boys continued to be hostile, Ben more than Steve. David had never been much good with children and he thought it was better to keep his distance.

Alice began to pay more attention to Winston than to David. That suited him. Life was easier without temptation. It didn't stop a pang of jealousy as he found a scantily clad Alice leaving Winston's room one morning.

Their situation was ideal; the property was secluded, almost impossible to find unless stumbled upon by accident. Solar power provided the means to cook without any tell-tale smoke to give them away. Food was available from an extensive vegetable patch, and rabbit and muntjac in the woods could be hunted almost silently by air rifle.

As long as they were careful not to make too much noise, they could realistically stay there for months. Nevertheless

David was constantly aware that he had a mission, and that was to get to the free zone and find Ruth. One day soon he was going to have to move on.

It had been drizzling lightly for several days now, so when it really started to rain, it came as a bit of a shock. The initial rat a tat tat of heavy raindrops on the windows made everyone jump, and then the heavens opened. The two young girls went over to the nearest window and peered out as the rainstorm developed into a deluge. Puddles began to form on the lawn, and the skies darkened. Winston got up from the table and walked to the window, looking over the heads of the girls at the storm.

"I don't think anyone's going to be wandering about outside with this lot going on, I think we can all take it easy for a few hours."

But a few hours turned into a day, then another, then a week. The garden was under inches of water. David occupied himself reading books that he found around the house, while Alice managed to amuse herself upstairs in the bedroom Winston had claimed as his own. David cursed himself for his earlier weakness with Alice, deciding that the pangs of jealousy over Winston served him right.

The girls and the two lads became quickly bored, and their squabbling and petty name calling began to get on everyone's nerves. David resolved that as soon as the storm had passed and things dried up a little he would leave the rest of them to it and continue on his quest. But his plan quickly went out of the proverbial window.

David had settled down in the big armchair in the kitchen, engrossed in a particularly interesting novel about a 1920s female detective. Winston and Alice were upstairs as usual, and the youngsters were all together in the front room.

David was of the opinion that as Winston had brought the youngsters with him, then it was up to him to keep them under control. The fact was, however, that no adult was really prepared to take on parental responsibilities, and so the kids were becoming uncontrollable.

The noise of arguing from the front room got louder and louder as an argument began to get out of hand. Suddenly, one of the girls started screaming, and Steve shouted at the other boy: "Ben! What the fuck have you done! You're bloody mad!"

David put his book down, got up, and walked to the bottom of the stairs. He listened, but neither Winston nor Alice seemed to be making any effort to come down and sort things out.

Now both girls were screaming, and David burst into the room.

One girl was sitting on the floor with her back to the wall, grasping her left arm with her right hand. Blood was seeping between her fingers, and a blood-covered knife lay next to her on the floor. The other girl was up against the window, looking terrified as Ben, standing in the middle of the room, pointed Alice's pistol at her. Steve was in the opposite corner curled up in a ball and shaking with fear as he tried to get away from the other boy.

As David entered the room, Ben swung around to face him, and the gun went off. The bullet shattered a small vase on a table about four inches to David's left. David lunged forward, and grabbed the gun; it went off a second time, putting a bullet hole high in the wall near the ceiling.

Winston and Alice came into the room. As David left, he slapped the gun into Winston's hand. "That's it! I'm not stopping in this mad house one minute longer!"

He stormed upstairs and grabbed his bag. As he began to stuff it with his clothes and with some that he had found in the house, Alice appeared in the doorway.

"Just think about what you're doing. You can't go off in this weather, its madness! Wait till you calm down."

David shouted back at her practically spitting out the words, "I am calm, just leave me alone."

Alice turned to leave the room. "I'll get my stuff and come with you."

David shouted after her: "No, stay here with your boyfriend!"

"Is that what this is all about? Me and Winston? You're in a mood about that?"

"Don't be silly Alice, I'm married, you can shag who you like."

Alice stormed off and shut herself in Winston's room, slamming the door behind her. Moments later, she reopened it to shout back at him: "You obviously didn't feel like that before they arrived!" Then she slammed the door behind her even harder.

David sat down on the bed; he couldn't understand how nearly being shot by a young boy had suddenly turned into an argument about Alice's sex life. He really did have to get out of there and get back to trying to find his wife. He stood and thought for a moment, and then dressed himself ready for the weather. Stopping outside Winston's door briefly, he thought about saying goodbye to Alice but then thought better of it. He left quietly through the back door and squelched across the lawn without looking back.

It wasn't long before he began to think that he may have been a bit hasty. The driving rain couldn't penetrate his waterproof outer clothing, but it still lashed at his exposed hands and face, and he was beginning to feel very uncomfortable.

He made his way back to the road and started his onward journey. It had been well after lunch when he had hastily taken his leave of the others, and he realised that he couldn't go much further in this downpour if he wanted any kind of a dry and comfortable night, and he was starting to get hungry.

In the distance he could just see an isolated house set a short distance back from the road. It was a lot closer to the highway than he would have liked, but given the appalling weather conditions he decided that he really had little choice, and that anyone out and about in this wouldn't be looking for fugitives.

The house was at the end of a short track, and David could see that most of the windows were broken. As he got nearer it became obvious that some sort of skirmish had taken place in and around the building. There were bullet holes around the front door frame, and the door itself was splintered where the lock should have been. He cautiously pushed the door back to reveal a large blood stain on the wooden floor; a number of used shot gun cartridges littered the hallway. There was no sign of bodies on the ground floor but a lot of the wooden furniture was damaged. Quietly as he could, he made his way upstairs two steps at a time - there was no evidence of any bodies up there, either.

One of the bedrooms showed signs of someone having used it, most probably after the violent event as there was no sign of a struggle in the room. There was an unmade bed, and cups and plates were strewn across the floor.

David decided that whoever had been there had most likely moved on, as there was no sign of dirty clothes - but in any case he had had enough of getting rained on for one day. If they came back he would deal with them then.

He removed his waterproofs and hung them on the back of a chair. Opting not to show a light or have a flame of any sort, he got out a packet of dry biscuits and a bottle of water, and settled down on the bed. He hadn't really exerted himself getting here, but his recent lack of exercise meant that he was not quite as fit as he had been. He soon became drowsy, and drifted off to sleep.

Something pressing on his forehead startled him into waking, and when he opened his eyes, he found himself staring down the barrel of an AK47. At its other end was a dishevelled old man with wild hair and an equally wild beard. Dawn was beginning to break and a dim light flooded the room. The man tapped him on the forehead again with the barrel, and David looked into the corner of the room where he had left his own gun.

"It's no good you looking for your piece, I've got it now. I'm the man with the gun now, and you're my bitch."

David looked into the wild eyes of his new acquaintance. "Look old boy, I don't want any trouble."

"Too late bitch, you're in big trouble now."

David tried to sit up but the old man again gave him a sharp tap on the top of his head. A plastic cable tie had been slipped over his wrist, and David found himself attached to the bedpost. Before he could move the old man tossed the AK47 onto the end of the bed and pulled David's free hand through another loop, securely handcuffing both hands to one side of the bed.

The scruffy old man shuffled backwards, and produced a large knife from his back pocket.

"You one of them heathens? Where's the rest of your tribe?"

"I can assure you…."

The man lunged forward before David could finish his sentence, and the tip of the large knife was terrifyingly close to his left eye.

"Shut the fuck up."

David waited for the old man to back away before trying again.

"I assure you sir, I'm the same as…." Before he could finish again the knife was thrust forward, this time nicking David's neck, blood trickled down to his shoulder.

"I said shut it or I'll carve you up."

Knowing now that the man was seriously unstable, David decided to keep quiet. The man backed off and started to pace up and down the room, barely audible but clearly talking to himself.

"He's come to kill me, they've sent him, there will be more, what to do, what to do."

He came at David again, slashing at David's chest and ripping open his shirt. He seemed to stop and think for a minute, then placed the point of the knife between the bottom two ribs on David's left hand side pushing just hard enough to draw blood.

"Cut his heart out and feed it to the pigs, he won't go to heaven. Then he can't hurt me no more."

David tried to speak, but the man clamped his free hand over his mouth.

"He'll scream when I stick him; his mates will be here in seconds. Better get something to gag him with."

Then he was up and out of the room. Minutes later he was back, by which time David was shaking uncontrollably with fear. The old man paced up and down again.

"Kill the bastard, kill the bastard, do it do it do it."

"Look man," David began again but quickly shut up as the old man glared at him. He'd not come all this way just to be murdered by some nutter. The pacing continued.

"We need to kill all the bastards, but how? Make him scream, that will make them come running. Yes that's it, make him scream."

He came towards David with the knife, and started cutting him slowly across the chest from shoulder to waist just deep enough to break the skin. David bit his lip to stifle the pain; the last thing he needed was a load of rebels bursting in. Everyone in the room would be trying to kill him then.

"Scream you bitch, I can hear your friends outside."

David thought it was the delusional rantings of an old man, but then he heard the creak of a door being pushed open downstairs. The old man dropped the knife, picked up the gun and pointed it towards the bedroom door. David considered shouting to warn them but decided whatever he did he was going to die in a hail of bullets. He tried to curl himself into the smallest ball possible and waited.

A single shot rang out and a pane of glass in the window shattered. The old man dropped the rifle and slowly sank to his knees, a large hole had appeared in the side of his head where the bullet had exited. He toppled onto his side, dead, and a large pool of blood formed around him on the floor.

After what seemed like an age, footsteps sounded on the stairs, slowly moving upwards. David braced himself and held his breath. A figure appeared in the doorway.

"Bloody hell David, can't you keep out of trouble for five minutes?"

Alice leaned on the door frame and smiled. David glared back at her.

"Where did you come from Alice? I thought you were stopping with your new friends."

"I said I'd come with you, why didn't you wait? I waited till this morning which was obviously far more sensible. When I saw this place and heard that old nutter raving, I guessed you would be involved somehow. I was listening downstairs when he was trying to make you scream, what was he doing? Pulling your hair?"

"No, he was bloody carving me up - can't you see I'm bleeding? Anyway, what took you so long?"

Alice went over to the bed and perched herself on the end.

"What, do you think I'm stupid? I wasn't going to come up the stairs. It took me a while to get outside and get a clear shot from on top of the shed roof."

Alice tugged at the ties binding him to the bed post.

"Oh I've got you now, just how I want you; I'm always up for a bit of bondage."

Alice began to unbuckle his belt as David tried to pull away from her.

"Come on Alice, stop mucking about, untie me."

DOG

"Bloody hell, Alice, you could be a bit gentler."

Alice had been dabbing away at the cuts across David's chest and neck with some cotton wool soaked in watered down disinfectant prior to applying some pretty large plasters. None of the cuts were very deep, but they were going to be sore for a couple of days.

"You're like a child, David, I have to follow you round everywhere just to keep you out of trouble and you still complain all the while."

"Why did you follow me anyway Alice? I thought you were happy with your new boyfriend."

She poked him in the ribs making him flinch.

"Will you pack it in with this jealousy crap? I only hooked up with Winston cause he had the biggest bed."

"Bullshit, biggest something else more like."

Alice got up and threw the cotton wool at him bouncing it off his head and went over to the little pan of water boiling away on the camping stove. She poured the water into a couple of pot noodles and left them to stand for a couple of minutes.

"I thought you and me were a team. Winston and his gang were just a diversion while we rested up for a couple of days, I started this trip with you and I fully intend to finish it with you. If you're worried about me meeting your wife don't, I'm not going to say anything."

"Alice, don't move."

She couldn't resist and turned to see what was behind her. Sitting in the doorway was a very large black Labrador staring intently at the two pot noodles.

"Careful, babe, he might be dangerous."

Alice moved towards the dog and spoke over her shoulder.

"You called me babe; you wanna be careful. People might get the wrong idea."

"Seriously though, it's probably not eaten for weeks, he might have your hand off."

As Alice got close to the dog it dropped to the floor and rolled over on its back, waving its front paws in the air as it waited for its tummy to be tickled.

Alice and the dog took to each other straight away; the dog was soon back up on his feet, thoroughly enjoying the scratching behind the ears he was getting from Alice. David was still concerned.

"You better not feed him, the last thing we need is a mutt following us around trying to get free meals."

Alice just ignored him and tipped one of the pot noodles out on to a relatively clean bit of floor. The dog wolfed it down in seconds, and sat staring lovingly at his new friends, as he licked his lips. David started to shuffle forward to the remaining pot of food.

"Well it looked like he enjoyed your breakfast and I hope you're not thinking of giving him mine?"

Alice quickly snatched it up.

"We can share it can't we, I thought we were going to help each other."

After their diminished breakfast the two of them packed their stuff away and got ready for the onward journey. There was no more need for waterproofs. The rain had stopped, and there were hints of sunshine poking through the clouds.

When everything was ready they cautiously made their way back to the road, deliberately ignoring the dog who had other ideas and decided to tag along. They walked in silence for the first couple of miles till Alice said

"I left Winston my handgun. I hope that was okay?"

"As long as he keeps it away from the kids it should be all right. He's probably in more danger from them than he is from the enemy. I've left the air rifle there anyway."

David had been trying to think of how they might complete the next stage of their journey and he had an idea that he thought might just work.

"I thought it might be a good idea to look for a boat."

GOVERNMENT IN EXILE

"Right - somebody give me some good news."

The members of the cabinet began to shuffle uncomfortably in their seats.

"Anyone? Anything?"

It had been two weeks since the British Government in exile had last convened to discuss the crisis, and the only significant thing that had happened was that they couldn't really call themselves the British Government anymore. Scotland had decided that they weren't part of the United Kingdom, and Northern Ireland had suddenly thought it was a good idea to be united with southern Ireland. The Home Secretary got to her feet.

"If anything, we appear to have even fewer friends than we did at our last meeting. The only new intelligence that we have that is verifiable, is that there are approximately eight SAS groups operating throughout the country and they are being coordinated by MI6 who have set up offices over here. There is one group in the south, probably a lone wolf that we are unable to contact, which is causing absolute mayhem down there.

"Our biggest concern is that if we manage to get the terrorists to the negotiating table, we won't be able to stop the lone wolf blowing up their supply trucks and harassing their personnel."

The PM gestured for her to sit down.

"Well, we can worry about that if the need arises. Anyone got anything else?"

The Education Secretary got to his feet.

"If I may, Prime Minister, the corridor across the country that was set up as a barrier between the two factions seems to be working quite well, neither side wanting to cause problems by entering it. Our information is that it's approximately ten to 20 miles wide and that any of 'our people' that manage to escape there are being left to themselves, though I'm sure the numbers of those escaping into the corridor are pretty minimal."

He sat down and the PM surveyed the room.

"Foreign Secretary, anything from you?"

"No, Prime Minister."

The PM glared at him.

"No. Is that it? Two weeks and all you can report is 'no'?"

"I have solicited help from all and sundry, PM Nobody wants to help, they're too scared of the same thing happening in their own countries."

"Well, I've been in touch with the US and they are putting a plan together to help, but I'm beginning to think the price we will have to pay will be too much. They're not very keen on invasions, given their track record. No point in re-convening unless something significant happens. Thank you, everyone."

TRAPPED

The rottweiler led the way; it padded through the short undergrowth of the woods closely followed by Ralph and Ruth carrying the bags of provisions between them. Their captors took up the rear, a short distance behind. Ralph kept looking to his left and right trying to maintain his bearings. Ruth looked straight ahead while trying to do the same thing.

"Just follow the dog. You don't need to know where you are, you're probably going to want to join up with us when you see our camp."

As they walked on in silence, Ralph reflected on the confrontation in the village. He understood that survivors would mistrust other groups that they came into contact with, but he was surprised how quickly things had descended into anarchy. These people obviously considered that anything in the immediate area belonged to them, and they were prepared to harm any outsiders who threatened their 'patch'. They had probably guessed from the amount of supplies he and Ruth were carrying that they were part of a bigger group. It was difficult to tell if they were being cautiously friendly towards the two of them right now, but things could easily turn violent.

After a while they came up to what could only be described as a wall of thick, apparently impenetrable vegetation. The dog walked along its perimeter, stopping at a gap that could only be seen when looking at it sideways on. The dog ducked under, and the group stooped to follow.

The other side was pretty much the same wooded area as they had come from, and they set off after the dog again. They were less than a mile back from the road, travelling parallel to it, but completely out of sight.

Suddenly a man armed with a shotgun stepped out from behind a tree and aimed the gun at Ralph's legs.

"Okay, hold it."

The man carrying Ralph's AK47 stepped forward.

"It's okay Jez, they're friendly."

They continued on until they came upon a clearing containing a number of what looked like four- or six-man tents, with probably a dozen men and women around a campfire.

One or two nodded in acknowledgement at the new arrivals, but no one spoke and most of the group seemed to ignore them. Their captors seated themselves on the large logs around the fire, indicating to Ralph and Ruth to do the same.

An elderly woman took a coffee pot off the fire and filled two cups. She half smiled as she gave one each to the newcomers.

"So where have you two come from, then"

Ruth nodded her thanks as she took the coffee.

"Me and Ralph have come up from the south, we've been hiding out for weeks, living off the land and generally keeping out of sight."

The old lady squatted in front of her and looked intensely into her eyes. "Just the two of you then?"

Ralph chipped in.

"There were four of us but we split up about a month ago, the other two seemed intent on looking for trouble."

"You can camp out with us if you want."

She indicated a couple of sleeping bags under a tarpaulin a short distance away from the tents. A meal was prepared mostly from the provisions that Ralph and Ruth had carried all the way to the camp. Very little was said during the meal, and they were not questioned further, although other members of the group seemed to regard the newcomers with suspicion.

As dusk began to fall, the fire was extinguished so that it wouldn't give away the camp's position. Ralph and Ruth moved over to their sleeping area, and spoke to each other in hushed voices.

"I don't like this Ralph, I'm reluctant to make friends with people who introduce themselves at gun point. All things considered I think it best if we keep them away from the rest of our group; this lot seem like the sort that would take everything we have."

"Yeah, and a larger group like this one stands more chance of detection. That one who seems to be in charge is a nasty bastard. They're obviously just trying to survive like the rest of us but there seems to be a power thing going on here."

"So Ralph, have you got any idea where we are, which is the way back, or where the horses are?"

"Yes I think so, but we'd better forget the horses if we're going to get away."

Ruth shook her head. "We can't leave them tied up, they'll starve to death, and they don't deserve that."

As it got darker, it was clear that there wouldn't be any light in the camp at all, as a precaution against being spotted by the enemy. Ruth and Ralph would have to wait until the moon came out if they were going to make their escape, and that didn't look very likely with the cloud cover as it was.

Suddenly, there was a large explosion, about two miles away. Unknown to the camp, Tommo had struck again. This time an ammunition truck had caught fire as it crashed - its driver had received a bullet to the head. After a short delay, sporadic gunfire broke out as the support troops from the ammunition trucks' escort convoy fired indiscriminately at buildings in the village, trying to locate the sniper.

The mayhem began to escalate as trigger-happy troops began to see imaginary enemy. Ralph gestured to Ruth to slowly move away from the camp and away from the source of all the noise. Camp members started to become very uneasy and congregated around the extinguished campfire. Inexplicably, the hunt for the marksman began to move into the woods, and nervous searchers began to fire randomly and at will into the wooded area.

As the camp dwellers began to arm themselves, Ruth and Ralph took the opportunity to slip into the darkening gloom, slowly at first, then breaking into a run when they were far enough away. They travelled as fast as they could along the wooded paths, jumping over fallen trees and bushes where it had become overgrown, and then suddenly they were out in the open. Ralph pulled Ruth to their left.

"Follow the tree line; we don't want to be caught in the open."

They again travelled as fast as they could, their progress made easier by being away from the undergrowth. Several shots suggested that the two sides had found each other back at the camp. Ruth and Ralph pressed on with determination.

When they arrived at a hedgerow running away from the woods at ninety degrees, Ralph tried to pull Ruth into a change of direction - but she was having none of it.

"The horses, we need to get the horses."

"It's too dangerous, Ruth, we need to start heading back to the farm."

She just ignored him and took off in the direction of the horses. Ralph hesitated for a moment, then shook his head and took off after her.

Two of the horses were still tethered where they had been left. Quickly, Ruth untied them and led them to a ditch to drink. The packhorse had managed to free itself from the tree it was tied to and had seemingly wandered off. It didn't have any tack on, so wouldn't arouse suspicion if anyone came across it.

Worried about being so close to the village, they stayed on foot and led the horses back to the hedgerow to follow it away from the woods. Progress was slow in the diminishing light but the sounds of gunfire were gradually left behind them.

Ruth began to tire from the exertion. "It must be safe to ride the horses now; we must be far enough away."

"If we get up on their backs we're going to be a couple of silhouettes that can be seen from miles away, safer as we are."

"Okay, but can we just stop for five minutes and catch our breath?"

The two of them slumped down and let the horses graze while they rested. Ruth peered into the night as the moonlight began to illuminate the countryside.

"Any idea where we are?"

Ralph thought about saying 'in the middle of nowhere' but sensing Ruth wasn't in the mood for sarcasm opted for a considered opinion.

"I think we are heading in the general direction of the farm but we would be lucky to go straight there. I remember it was in a dip, so we might not even see it and go straight past."

Ruth stood up and peered over the fence. "Best if we keep going till we get to that road that leads to the farm drive and see if we can get our bearings from there."

The gunfire from the woods had died down, with only the occasional single shots ringing out. Ralph feared that what they could hear were executions, which filled him with a greater sense of urgency.

"We had better get back to the farm as quick as we can in case they start to widen the search area."

With that, they got to their feet and again began to lead the horses on. After a while they came across a road that had to be the road to the farm.

Ruth looked left and right. "Okay, so which way?"

"Your guess is as good as mine, you choose."

Ruth set off to the left and Ralph followed.

"If we don't find it in ten minutes we better turn back and try the other way."

They were a lot closer than they had thought, and within just a few minutes, they came across the entrance to the farm drive.

There, Ralph handed the reins of his horse to Ruth.

"Wait with the horses the other side of the road, behind that high hedge. Bob and the others won't be expecting us from this direction, and there's no point in us both getting shot at."

Ruth crossed the road with the horses as Ralph made his way down the drive. He kept well away from the hedgerow and out in the moonlight so that their companions would be able to see him approaching. He disappeared out of sight at the end of the drive but returned minutes later, gesturing to Ruth to come on down. As she made her way up to the farm, she was met by Sophie who helped her take the horses to the stable, remove the saddles and feed and water the two hunters.

Everyone was keen to know why Ralph and Ruth had been away so long. They told their story, taking it in turns to fill in the details. Bob and the rest of the girls listened in silence. When they had finished, Ralph thought that he had better warn everyone.

"There's a danger the occupying forces will send out search parties in the morning to catch anyone who may have escaped. I think we should prepare ourselves here, it's got to be better than being caught out in the open."

Bob indicated his rifle propped up against the chimney breast.

"We're down to two shooters; we won't be able to put up much of a fight."

Ralph had forgotten that his and Ruth's guns had been taken by their new 'friends'.

"It depends how many there are when they come looking. We'll have to improvise some weapons and lay a few traps. Let's look around and see what we can find."

The kitchen provided a few knives, but Bob was unconvinced that any of the girls apart from Ruth would be capable of using them. Ralph had noticed a gun cabinet in the spare room upstairs, but knowing farmers, he was reluctant to spend time and energy breaking into it until he had checked the attic.

Sure enough, just inside the hatch he found a loaded twelve bore and a box of cartridges - farmers always liked to have a gun where they could get hold of it easily. The decision was made that the girls armed with knives would hide themselves in three pairs around the farm, while Ralph, Bob and Ruth would have the guns and position themselves where they could intervene in any confrontation.

After checking that they were all clear about the plan, Bob volunteered to keep lookout for the night. Everyone apart from Bob settled down and tried to get a little sleep.

Everyone but Ruth was awake again before dawn, finding it impossible to sleep for fear of what the morning might bring. Ruth, hardened by what she had seen and experienced, and dog tired from the adventures of the previous day, slept on.

Everyone congregated in the kitchen, and Ralph tried to rustle up a simple breakfast when Ruth eventually joined them.

Ralph addressed the group. "Okay, let's remind ourselves of the plan. You ladies need to pair up. I suggest Shirley and Jean hide in the house. In the attic is probably the best place, but you can just stay upstairs until something happens. Imogen and Nadia, I'm going to make a cosy little hideaway behind a load of bales in the hay store - you should be pretty safe there. Sophie and Mary, you can hide in the stables - that dead horse is still in there, and it should deter any prying eyes."

One or two of the group tried to eat breakfast, but most were too nervous, and worried about throwing up.

As the sun started to rise, Ralph went out to find himself somewhere he could observe the road without being seen.

The plan was for the three with guns to position themselves in the hedgerows and ditches so that they could bring their guns to bear if they needed to.

Everything depended on how many came to search the place, and how thorough they would be. A fire fight would surely attract the attention of others nearby, and nobody wanted that. In the event of a confrontation, they would have to be able to relocate pretty quickly.

With this in mind, everyone packed their stuff into bags ready to leave. These would be kept behind the bales of hay where Imogen and Nadia were going to be hiding.

The morning dragged on. They had split into two groups, four of the girls in the hay barn next to the stables, and the rest, apart from Ralph, in the house. There was a moment of panic when gunshots were heard from the direction of the village, but then everything went quiet again.

Just after midday, the moment they had feared arrived. Ralph came into the house.

"Okay, there are a couple of trucks but they've just stopped at the farmhouse on the other side of the road. I don't think there can be any doubt that we're next."

No one said anything, just moved to their positions as quietly as they could. Bob, keeping out of sight of the road, made his way across to the barn to warn the girls over there. The wait seemed interminable. Nobody dared move in case of discovery.

Nearly an hour later, the two vehicles made their way down the long drive. They were Toyota Hilux-type vehicles, and the second in line had a large calibre machine gun mounted on the back. Three men dressed head to toe in black were in each truck. They stopped in the courtyard between the house and the stables, and waited. Both doors opened on both trucks and six men poured out, meeting in a group between the two vehicles. Cigarettes were passed and lit, and loud chatter could be heard.

Coming to a decision, five of the men reached into the back of the trucks to retrieve semi-automatic weapons. The sixth man stayed with the truck with mounted machine gun. He settled down in the back, looking as if he fully intended to relax, as this was the tenth farm they had done today without incident, and he was getting pretty bored. The others split into two groups, and went off to explore the farm.

Ruth, unaware of any of this, had positioned herself on the opposite side of the stable so she would have a good view of where the other girls were hiding. Bob was on the far side of the house, ready to deal with any trouble in the house itself. Ralph was on top of an old shipping container which provided him with a view of most of the farm area.

Two men went to the house, unnecessarily kicking the front door in; they could be heard inside, smashing crockery and generally wrecking the place just for fun. The other three walked through the hay barn and only gave a cursory look at the stacked bales.

It was obvious they were not taking their job very seriously. They had no intention of searching for something that they didn't think was there. They didn't even bother to keep their guns at the ready, opting instead to keep them slung over their shoulders. Only the lead man toyed with an automatic pistol as he walked through the building. Stopping at the entrance to the stable, the stench of the decomposing horse hit them. Two them turned to go, but the third pointed to the far end.

"Come on, it's not that bad, and we can get out the other end. Quicker than going all the way round."

He pulled the neck of his tee shirt up over his nose and pressed on; the other two followed him doing the same. As they reached the far end they passed the stable that Mary and Sophie had hidden in.

Racked with fear, Sophie gave out a barely audible repeated whimper. The man with the pistol turned back and slowly pushed the stable door open. Sophie was out of sight behind the stable framework but Mary was left in full view. She slowly stood up. Even without his heavily strapped-up leg, Mary would have recognized him as the young man whose life she had pleaded for.

"Sonny."

Without hesitation he raised his pistol and shot Mary right between the eyes.

Whether it was revenge for the murder of his lifelong friend, or embarrassment in front of his colleagues that this woman knew him, Mary would never know. She lay on the stable floor, dead, in a growing pool of her own blood.

Ruth was about ten yards away and out of sight when the two men with Sonny backed out of the stable block. She stepped into the open and fired both barrels of her shotgun, killing one instantly and severely injuring the other. Seeing his companions on the ground, Sonny moved towards the middle of the stables.

Having realized that everything was kicking off, Bob ran towards the house arriving just as the two in the house came running out. A long burst of fire from his AK47 put paid to them both.

Ralph, unable to see what had happened in the barn, rapidly climbed down off the shipping container. When he arrived at the entrance to the stables, Sonny had his back to him. Ralph cut him down with a burst of fire before Sonny could turn around.

That left the man in the truck who picked up his rifle and stood up, but before he could jump to the ground his head exploded and his body fell back into the truck. Neither Ralph nor Ruth could have shot him from their positions and Bob was out of sight behind the farm house.

Back in the tree line, having no need to worry about giving away his position with all that was happening, Tommo began to pack away his sniper rifle. He was pleased with the shot; it was a good half mile, and the target was limited by the side of the building obstructing half the truck. He was reassured by the way the two men were looking around trying to establish where the shot had come from that all the hostiles had been dealt with. He didn't think it necessary to introduce himself to the party, and he melted away into the woods.

ALICE AND DAVID

Alice and David walked most of the next day. The dog was now their constant companion. They kept themselves in the countryside as much as they could, avoiding main roads and skirting around villages, opting not to investigate unless completely necessary.

Aware that they were going to need food, they kept a close lookout for any remote farms or houses, but when there was any sign of human activity they steered clear. Even in empty places where there was no visible sign of life, Alice would rummage about inside while David, standing guard, would break into a cold sweat.

Entry was usually from a back door or window that had been left open, probably down to a lack of security consciousness rather than the current crisis. Alice would concentrate on the kitchen and retrieve what canned provisions she could find. Dried goods like rice and pasta were also a welcome addition. Bottled water was a bonus in case the tap water system failed. She had perfected her search technique to the point that she could be in and out in less than five minutes, much to David's relief.

Towards the end of the following day they found themselves close to the summit of a hill. They stopped to heat up something to eat before the light faded and the flame from the little gas cooker could give away their position.

In the distance they could see a large, populated area that didn't look, from their vantage point, to have been affected by the hostilities. David pointed towards it with his spoon.

"That must be Wolverhampton; we definitely need to avoid that. The guards in my camp said it was a massive stronghold for the occupying forces. Some of the guards were from there. Tomorrow we need to head towards Bridgnorth, which I reckon is over there."

This time the spoon was pointed away to his right.

"We'll probably have to skirt round that as well, although it's nowhere near as big."

After consuming a meal of pasta spirals, tinned ham and pea soup, they each bedded down in a single person tent ready for a good night's sleep. The dog had become a great asset; it happily slept outside under a little canvas lean-to that they erected for it. At the first sign of anything coming or happening out of the ordinary, it would emit a low growl, and would only bark if it sensed real danger. David and Alice could get a good night's sleep secure in the knowledge that the dog would keep a look out for any unwelcome visitors.

Next morning they set off in the direction David had suggested. Progress was good until, that afternoon, they came through a gap in a hedge, only to be confronted by a canal with no visible means of crossing in either direction. David pointed to his left.

"I'm guessing that this runs all the way into Wolverhampton and we don't want to get too close to that."

Alice looked disgusted. "Don't tell me we are going to be heading in exactly the opposite direction to where we want to get to?"

"It'd be safest Alice; we don't want to run into trouble if we can help it."

The dog had already decided that turning right would be the best course of action, so Alice set off after the dog.

"It looks like the land rises up this way so there's got to be a lock."

About ten minutes later, the dog had gone ahead and was out of sight around a bend. Alice stopped. "Listen! The dog."

They could hear the dog's deep growling, indicating trouble, and they both edged slowly forward. A narrowboat came into view. The dog was sitting on the bank, staring intently at the bow. The double doors into the cabin were closed and the windows down the side of the boat had curtains drawn.

David gestured to Alice and they both walked backwards, back around the bend, until the boat was once again out of sight. Shrugging off their back packs and coats, they checked their AK47s. David spoke in hushed tones.

"We get on the back of the boat as quietly as we can. You pull the door open - it looks like the lock has been broken - and I'll jump in."

Alice nodded and, guns at the ready, they began to edge back towards the boat.

Slowly and steadily they climbed on at the bow. "David, be careful."

Alice pulled the door open, and David jumped into pitch darkness inside. He moved forward, and fell over a body on the floor, which let out a loud groan.

Hearing no gun shots, Alice followed inside and pulled back the first set of curtains to reveal David lying on the floor next to a man flat on his back holding his stomach, with blood covering his shirt and fingers. Alice tried to lift the man's hand to see the extent of the bleeding, but he resisted.

"David, get me a sheet off one of those beds, let's see if we can bandage him up."

Alice tried to put a dressing on his stomach wound but as she tried to pass the ripped sheet underneath his body, it became obvious that he had a large exit wound in his back. She looked at David and shook her head. The man started to come round.

"The bastards got me, left me for dead."

Alice looked around but could see no signs of any fighting on the boat. "Where were you?"

"Couple of miles back, they caught me as I tried to cross the M54, it's a real bastard. So much traffic I'd actually got across and turned round to see if anyone was following when they shot me."

David put a cushion under the man's head in a bid to make him a little more comfortable.

"How did you get here, to this boat?"

"I walked. They didn't follow, don't really know how I kept going, adrenalin I guess. I came across this narrowboat and broke in, couldn't have gone any further, that's why I collapsed on the floor."

Alice gave him a sip of water from a bottle on the table. "So where were you trying to get to?"

"I was heading for Holyhead eventually, try to get a boat to Ireland, I've got family there."

David was trying to peer out the window to make sure things were safe. "How far had you come?

"Oxford, I was in a camp down there before I escaped."

"So did you come through the neutral zone, does it exist?"

"Yeah it exists all right, follows the rivers, the Severn up to Tewkesbury then the Avon to Stratford then another that I forget the name of and right across to the East coast. Anyway it's about 20 miles wide and both sides keep out of it."

The man started to sound weaker, his breathing became laboured, his face covered in sweat. Alice dabbed his face with a towel. "Try to get some sleep; you've lost a lot of blood."

Alice and David made their way up to the far end of the boat out of earshot of the dying man. Alice wiped the blood off her hands with the towel.

"He's not going to last very long, he's bleeding to death. Look, if we untie the boat, do you think it might drift to the other bank?"

"Well it's worth a try, I'm sure we can give it a bit of persuasion. It's not going to drift far towards Wolverhampton - there's no current cos it's a canal."

Alice looked offended. "Yes I know that, we just need to get the other side."

They fetched their gear from back around the bend, and when they returned the man was dead. David wrapped him in a sheet and put him onto the bed; they got the dog on board and untied the mooring ropes.

Using the bargepole from the roof, they managed to push the vessel so it drifted to the opposite bank. There they disembarked, and headed for the problematic M54. They hadn't learnt the man's name, but there was nothing they could do for him now.

Progress on the opposite side of the canal was slow; they had become more cautious than ever, avoiding all but the most minor of roads. As dusk fell they made camp in a small thicket, preparing and eating their evening meal before darkness as usual. A light rain began to fall, and Alice tutted under her breath.

"We should have stopped on the boat. We're going to get soaked if this gets any heavier."

"I don't know about you, Alice, but I wasn't keen on spending the night with a dead body."

As she crawled into her tent the dog got in with her.

"At least the dog will keep you warm in the night."

When David crawled out of his tent the next morning, Alice handed him a cup of steaming hot tea and half a packet of digestive biscuits.

"There you go, that should give you plenty of energy for the morning stroll."

And then, as he began to munch on his biscuits, she added "How the hell are we going to get across this motorway?"

David finished his biscuit, broke another in half, and popped that into his mouth. Alice gestured with her palms upwards. "Well?"

"I'm thinking."

He sprayed crumbs in her general direction.

"I think we need to walk up to the motorway and gauge how much traffic there is. If our recently deceased friend is correct, we don't want to be walking alongside it looking for a crossing - that would be suicidal."

They broke camp and headed directly for the motorway. It wasn't long before they heard the noise of traffic. When it was in sight, they could see that the man hadn't been exaggerating. The M54, a two-lane motorway between the Midlands and Wales, was as busy as it had been before the war. Today's traffic was a mix of military vehicles, lorries and a smattering of private cars. David shook his head in despair.

"It should peter out a bit past Telford, but we don't want to have to go all the way past there. There's got to be a footbridge, surely? We need to go back into the countryside and track across till we find a minor road that will take us across."

Half an hour later, walking parallel to the motorway but about a mile back from it, they came across an 'A' road. It took a while, but eventually there was enough of a lull in the traffic for them to cross it.

Another two hours of walking, and they found what they were looking for, a single track road heading in the direction of the motorway. Still taking every precaution, they followed the road till they came to the bridge across the motorway.

They settled themselves out of sight, in a nearby field, and waited for dusk.

Darkness came, but the volume of traffic only started to lessen noticeably around one o'clock in the morning. By two o'clock, when there was only one vehicle every couple of minutes or so, they decided to venture across.

Keeping to the centre of the bridge, they crouched as low as possible, and made slow progress. Whenever traffic approached, they dropped to their knees.

Once across the bridge, they rested their aching knees for 10 minutes, and then set off again into the countryside. A lack of moonlight made continuing dangerous - this was an unkempt road, full of potholes, so they settled down to rest until dawn.

After a couple of hours fitful sleep, they were underway again, and passed a deserted football stadium, Shifnal Town FC.

"We can't be very far from the town," said David. "We need to keep going south till we pick up the River Severn just past Bridgnorth."

It was another five hours before they managed it. Later on they would look for a boat, but in the meantime they hid in woods.

RUTH'S GROUP

Ralph ran over to the truck and pulled the almost headless body off the back by its feet. Bob ran to the barn and called to the girls as he gathered up as much of the baggage as he could carry.

"Come on you lot, we need to get out of here sharpish. Grab your stuff and mount up, four to a truck."

Jean began to walk back to where Mary had fallen. "We can't just leave her, it's not right."

Bob went after her and grabbed her by the elbow. "She's dead. There's nothing you can do, and we need to get out of here."

Minutes later the two trucks and all the survivors powered up the drive and swung out onto the road. Ralph drove the lead vehicle as fast as he felt he could safely along the narrow country road, closely followed by Bob driving the other which was harder to handle with its large machine gun on the back. Sophie was sitting in the passenger seat, sobbing.

Bob assumed that the plan was to put as much distance as possible between themselves and the farm before abandoning the vehicles. The trick was to do this without being seen.

Ralph suddenly skidded to a halt almost catching Bob unawares. He had spotted a single track road to the left. Ralph turned up it and again gunned the truck as fast as he dared, and the little convoy raced along for a couple of miles. Ralph braked again, but Bob was ready for him this time, and they both swung up a dirt track that headed for some woods. Ralph was concerned by the dust that the two vehicles were kicking up, but they were soon deep into the trees and he slowed the pace.

After he had travelled as far as he could without coming out the other side, he pulled off the track and pressed forward till the truck was stuck in the undergrowth. Bob followed suit. Everyone jumped out of the two trucks, retrieved their baggage, and formed a rough circle around Ralph.

"Okay everyone, we need to get as far away as we possibly can. It will probably mean walking well into the night if you're up to it. Hopefully it will be a while before they come looking for us."

Ruth looked concerned. "I think one of them might still be alive, he was groaning when we left but he was losing a lot of blood."

"Why the hell didn't you finish him off?"

Ruth was surprised to hear that this was coming from Sophie, and Bob stepped in before an argument developed.

"He's probably not going to be able to tell them anything, and it's no good worrying about it now. Did anyone see who shot the last man in the back of the truck?"

They looked at each other, and shook their heads. Ralph broke the silence. "Let's not worry about that now. Like I said, we need to get the hell out of here and as far away as possible."

Ralph took the lead and the small party began their long trek. As they left the woods, lights were just coming on in the city in front of them. It looked like it was a sprawling and busy place.

"That must be Oxford. We need to give it a wide berth. If we can get round the city and put it way behind us before we break for a sleep, we might have a chance."

Bob nodded in agreement. "It's a good plan. If we can get to Woodstock on the other side of Oxford, we should be able to rest a couple of days in the grounds of Blenheim. There's bound to be plenty of empty buildings there."

Everyone marched in single file behind Ralph. No one seemed to be in any mood for conversation. As the hours passed, they made good ground, and by the middle of the night Oxford had been left far behind.

Making camp in a small coppice well away from any roads, each got into a sleeping bag on the ground - it was too dark to pitch tents, and they couldn't risk showing any torchlight.

They had managed to cross the only main road which could have blocked their way, so progress the following day was relatively leisurely.

The grounds of Blenheim Palace lay in front of them, and as they made their way towards the main house, it became clear that the Palace had not come through the hostilities unscathed. Bomb craters lay along the drive, and tank tracks had cut up furrows in the grass.

Getting nearer to the house, they could see all the windows were broken; and as their view of the building changed it was clear that a quarter of the building had been destroyed.

They entered the undamaged part of the building through a side entrance, as quietly as they could - the crunch of broken glass underfoot made that difficult. Furniture, once priceless, was now broken and littered the floors. Artworks on the walls were either shredded or missing.

Bob walked up to an empty space on the wall where a picture had hung until recently. "So, some of the stuff has been stolen, and some of it's vandalized?"

A voice behind them answered: "Yes, that's correct."

Everyone spun round, and those with guns pointed them at the figure in the doorway. He was a middle aged man of stocky build, in a khaki boiler suit, with his hands in his pockets. Ruth lowered her shotgun. "And who might you happen to be?"

"Well I happen to be the head groundkeeper, or at least I used to be. Not a lot of point now."

"But you're still here - why is that?"

The man moved deeper into the room. "I'm George, by the way; we'll get to your names later."

He hitched himself up on to an eighteenth century occasional table over by the wall and swung his legs back and forth.

"When the war started they pretty much left this place alone, no strategic value I should imagine. We didn't have much of a clue what was going on. As you know there was a great lack of information. But we took the decision to try and pack up some of the artworks and store them in a place of safety. As you can see, we didn't manage to save it all before a couple of tanks and half a dozen people carriers turned up. I don't think culture was their thing, really. Fortunately none of us were around, so they didn't know we were still here."

Ralph interrupted him. "You keep saying 'we', are there more of you?"

"Yeah, there's a dozen of us altogether. I'll introduce you in a minute and you'll see why they couldn't find us."

He went over to the door. "I take it you didn't see any hostile troops around on your way here?"

He looked at Bob, who shook his head, then held up his hand in a gesture that told them all to wait. A faint hum gradually got louder as a helicopter approached and flew overhead. After it had passed and faded into the distance, George jerked his head to tell them to follow.

Filing out the door, they followed George down a path through wooded gardens, and down to the butterfly house which, as they noticed, had been turned into a sort of hot house market garden. Cutting across a small lawn, they came to what the sign said was the Marlborough Hedge Maze, and George waited for everyone to catch up.

"Keep close to me, you can actually get lost in here."

Just before they reached the entrance to the centre of the maze, George stopped and took a large key from his back pocket. Reaching down, he pulled up a manhole cover to reveal a staircase running down into the depths. Reaching down with his foot he clicked on a light switch to light the way, and held out his hand to Jean to guide her to the first step. Single file, they descended two flights of staircase which ended in a passageway. This sloped downwards in the general direction of where, above ground, the main house would be. George closed the manhole cover behind him before he too descended the stairs.

"Just walk down the tunnel, you'll be fine."

Ralph pushed his way to the front and began to lead the party along the tunnel. As they moved forwards, lights in the ceiling came on automatically to light their way, until eventually they stopped at a large metal door.

For the first time since they had encountered George, Ralph began to feel uneasy, and as unobtrusively as he could he slipped his AK47 off his shoulder. George moved to the side of the door, and punched a succession of numbers into a keypad. The door swung open, inwardly.

Ahead of them was a similar door. Once the whole group was through, George closed the first door behind him. Ralph's finger hovered around the trigger guard of his gun. He jumped when he felt George's hand on his shoulder. "Don't worry pal, it's just a precaution, I'll soon have us inside."

The second door was at least six inches thick, but it swung open with ease after George entered a code into the second keypad. A short corridor opened up into a room the size of two tennis courts, with doors every six feet or so around the walls.

Seven men and three women sat at tables in groups, and as the party entered the room they all got up and came to greet the newcomers. Everyone talked at once trying to introduce themselves; seats were offered at the tables, and plates of food were brought out for everyone.

Ralph carefully placed his weapon on an empty table. As hungry as he was, he had no desire to eat until he knew more about their circumstances. George noticed the look of concern on his face and went over to reassure him. "Would you like me to show you around my friend?"

George and Ralph made their way towards one of the many doors in the wall.

"When the war started we were untouched initially and, like you I suspect, we didn't have a clue what was going on. That first day some of the staff, mostly the married ones, went home. We never saw any of them again. The rest of us came down here. By the next day it had become obvious that something serious was happening, and that's when we started to store the artwork in the vaults under the house. On the third day the tanks came, and we were still all down here. They must have been able to see that there was no one in the main house or the grounds and they just shot the place up for fun."

"And have you been down here ever since?"

George smiled. "Pretty much. We can get out though; we're growing vegetables in the butterfly house so we take it in turns to spend half a day in there."

George opened a door to reveal what was the communications room, with a bank of screens covering the end wall.

"As you probably know this is the ancestral home of the Churchills. These underground vaults were converted during the second world war when MI5 was stationed here.

Subsequently it was updated to be used as a control centre should anything like what's just happened occur. We can monitor the grounds from in here; that's how we knew you were around. All the cameras are well hidden. No one would find them if they didn't know where to look."

He steered Ralph towards the door.

"MI5 were caught unawares like the rest of us, so we took the place over ourselves."

Ralph entered the room and nodded at a man sitting in front of the monitors. George introduced the two men, who shook hands.

"Colin is attempting to monitor the airwaves, but so far he's heard nothing of any use. We do have the capability to transmit but we don't want to give away the fact that someone's here."

George and Ralph left the room and shut the door behind them. George led the way to the next room.

"We're completely self-sufficient here; we could survive for a year without going outside. There's a deep well that provides us with water, and some recycling composters and compacters, that sort of thing, to deal with waste. Power comes from solar panels on the roofs of some of the outbuildings. They're only visible from the air, and they are disguised to look like corrugated roofing."

He held open the next door into a room that resembled two long aisles of a supermarket. "Tinned supplies."

He shut it again.

"There's an air circulation system which is again disguised on the surface, so plenty of fresh air."

The next room was a dormitory with four large cubicles. "There are 10 of these so there's enough room for 40 people to sleep in comfort."

George pointed to another door. "Games room, snooker, table tennis, darts and a couple of cross trainers."

When they returned to the main group, they found them filing into a room at the far side. It was a lounge, with a number of settees and armchairs scattered about, and a large projection screen at one end.

"You and your party are welcome to stay as long as you like", George said.

Ralph called his group together at one end of the lounge, and their new hosts backed away to a respectful distance.

"Okay, George has invited us to stay for as long as we like. Ruth, I know you're going to want to move on sooner rather than later, but I would suggest that we give it a week and then reassess who wants to move on."

There was a general murmur of approval as Ralph waited for any sign of dissent. "They've got hot showers as well..."

Shirley could hardly contain a squeal of delight. Rooms were allocated with the girls taking two; Ralph and Bob took two cubicles in another. George had invited them to share the one that he occupied alone but understood that they might want a little privacy until they got to know people better.

Ralph and Bob had hardly got settled in when there was a tapping at the door. Bob slowly got up and went to open it. "Ruth."

"Have you got a minute? There's something I wanted to discuss."

Ralph got out of his bed and came to the entrance of his cubicle. "We were just going to take a shower, won't it keep?"

"Well yes, it's not that important, I just wondered what you thought about what happened back at the farm. The sniper who saved us - he was obviously highly trained. He ought to be told about this place really."

With that she left, shutting the door behind her.

Later, when everyone had showered, got a change of clothes, and had a good rest, they all met back in the dining area. Three of the men were busy preparing the evening meal, and Imogen and Nadia went over to offer to help. There was a lot of light hearted chatter as everyone set about making friends.

Ralph went and found Ruth, and joined her at a separate table. "What did you mean earlier about that sniper?"

"Well, I have been thinking. It might have been him that set off the commotion in the village where we got captured; and whoever he is, he was definitely trying to look out for us at the farm. I think he's probably SAS or something similar, and he's on a mission to cause as much disruption as possible."

"You're probably right Ruth, but we wouldn't be much help to him."

"Yeah I know that, but he's probably got hundreds of the enemy out looking for him, and his luck will only hold out for so long. If he could have somewhere like this, somewhere they would never find him, as a base, then he would probably be able to operate for months. And anyway, I think we owe him."

"But if the terrorists can't find him, what chance have we got?"

"I don't know, Ralph, but I think we ought to try."

The rest of the evening was very relaxed. Some went to bed early after their long march, but the rest stayed in the lounge late into the night. Jean and Ralph enjoyed relating their exploits to a captive audience.

Next morning, after breakfast, Ruth asked George if it was okay to go to the Comms room. There she took a seat next to Paul, who was the operator for that day.

"When you're monitoring the wireless signals, Paul, can you pick up when there's been any trouble? I'm thinking there is a sniper disrupting road traffic by attacking trucks or convoys."

"Well, the voices I hear do stick to English till they get excited, then I can't understand a word they're saying."

Ruth noticed a large open notebook on the desk. "Do you keep a record of anything that you hear?"

Paul handed her the book. "Anything we can make sense of, we write in here."

Ruth turned the page back to the previous day but saw nothing of interest, just a list of people checking in with their control centre in Oxford. She turned the page to the day of the confrontation at the farm, and was a little surprised that there was no mention of anything happening there - but she thought this couldn't be taken to mean they didn't know about it, or hadn't found the carnage that they had left.

Flicking over the page again, she found what she had been looking for. Halfway down the page there was reference to anyone available being asked to converge on the village of Flyfield. She was pretty sure she had read 'Flyfield Village Hall' on the plaque outside the hell hole they discovered where the children had been hanged.

"Paul, do you know who made this entry?"

"Yeah, Richard, I think."

Ruth went to the doorway and shouted:

"Which one of you is Richard?"

A lad in his mid-twenties got up from the dining table and made his way over to Ruth. At the doorway, he finished off the chocolate bar he was eating. "That's me, what can I do for you?"

"Did you write this?"

Richard took the book from her hands and studied it closely. "Yep, sure did."

"Can you remember if the word sniper was used?"

"Now you come to mention it, yes I reckon it was."

Ruth thanked him, put the book back on the desk, and went to look for Ralph who was still at a table nursing a cup of coffee; she scooted in beside him and nudged him with her elbow.

"I know how we can find him, our friend the sniper."

"You sure you want to do this Ruth? I thought you wanted to get to your husband."

"I do, but this is really important, this is the only person we've come across who's putting up some sort of resistance. I think it's important we do something to help him."

Ruth outlined her plan - to monitor the radio transmissions to find where he attacks next, then go out to the same area and hope that he spotted them before the enemy did.

"It's a bloody thin plan, Ruth, you could get us both killed."

"You're going to come with me then?" She smiled.

The day passed without incident. A couple of the girls joined the party out tending to the vegetables in the butterfly house, and the games room was fully occupied throughout the day. Nearly everyone came together in the afternoon to watch a movie on the large screen in the lounge.

The Comms room was manned 24 hours a day, and Ruth spent some time in there familiarizing herself with the set up. The attack in Flyford had taken place just before dusk, so Ruth reasoned that the sniper picked this time so he didn't have to wait long for darkness when he could slip away undetected. It was the evening transmissions that she was particularly interested in, and so she volunteered to do that shift.

She took her evening meal at the desk, and then, just when the cameras switched to infra-red and the screens turned to black and white, there was suddenly a lot of activity on the radio waves. Anyone available was being ordered to the main road just outside Woodstock. As Ruth glanced up at the screens, she noticed on one of them the glow of what looked like a fire in the distance.

Attracted by her shouts, Ralph came to the doorway. "What's up?"

She pointed up to the screen. "That's our man. I'm sure of it, he's taken something out on the Oxford Road, not far from here."

"Let's hope it don't bring people here looking for him."

Ruth began gathering her stuff up from the desk. "Can you take over here? I need to get out there and make contact with him."

"You can't go out there, Ruth, you'll put everyone in here in danger. Leave it till things blow over - he'll still be around if they don't catch him."

Ruth tried to push past him.

"You're not going out there, I'll lock you up if I have to."

She shrugged her shoulders and sat back down. She monitored the radio deep into the night and could tell by the tone of the messages that the sniper had yet to be located. Then, about two o'clock in the morning, everything began to quieten down and Ruth guessed that he had slipped through the net once again.

Her attention now shifted to the monitors in case he decided to make his escape across the estate, and she was only really half listening to the radio when it all kicked off again. The sniper had apparently been spotted near Wootton, a village on the same road but further north. All available units were ordered to switch to searching in that area.

Ruth was not convinced. From what she knew about this chap, he wouldn't be careless enough to be spotted twice in one night. In fact he wasn't spotted the first time - they only knew he was there because he'd taken out his target.

Paul came to take over in the Comms room for the rest of the night. Ruth went and got her head down, aiming for just a couple of hours' sleep. In fact, she overslept, and everyone else was up eating breakfast when she woke.

Her first act was to head for the Comms room. "Morning Paul. Anything happening?"

"A lot of chatter on the radio till it went quiet about five. Nothing on the screens, no movement at all. The chopper has been over a couple of times though."

Ruth left him and went to get some breakfast; she found a seat next to Ralph. "Am I allowed out this morning to see if there's any sign of him? If he is as good as I think he is he will find me once I'm out there."

It was nearly midday when Ruth got outside. There had been no action or movement all morning. George let her out and guided her to the edge of the maze before hiding in the entrance to wait for her return. She was armed with a hand gun and Bob's AK47, and made her way to the outbuildings.

Once there she was pretty well shielded by trees or large bushes all the way to the house, apart from when she had to crouch and run through the Italian Garden with its lower hedges.

It was quickly obvious to her that it would not be possible for her to enter the house through the badly damaged side, so a diversion around to the front had to be made. Once inside it was easy to get up to the first floor, and there she positioned herself at a window with a reasonable view of the immediate surroundings.

Ruth had been at the window for nearly an hour. She was sure from her vantage point that she would see anyone in the grounds or attempting to enter the house - so the little cough she heard from behind her made her go cold. Turning round, she saw a bearded man camouflaged from head to foot and holding a large telescopic rifle across his chest with his two hands. She couldn't believe that she hadn't heard him approach, as there was broken glass and rubble all over the floor. He spoke with a deep, hushed voice. "Hello."

It sounded so absurd that Ruth nearly laughed out loud, but just smiled instead. "I didn't hear you come in."

She stood up and approached him. "I'm Ruth; you must be the sniper who's been causing all the mayhem. I thought I might be able to spot you if you were in the area. I should have known you're not that easy to find as you've escaped detection this long."

Tommo grinned back at her.

"You're a little too easy to spot, Miss, you need to be careful. I've been tracking your party since back at the farm."

Ruth explained the set up at the underground bunker and invited him to stay; he was naturally reticent but agreed to take a look. George was waiting for them when they reached the maze, and Tommo began to relax a little when he was introduced to the other residents. He accepted Ruth's idea of using the bunker as a base, but said he would go out on week-long missions to lessen the chances of leading undesirables back to the estate. Tommo settled into his own room, but his gun was always within reach.

IN EXILE

"Is this it then? Just the four of us?"

"Yes Prime Minister, most of the others have taken...."

The P.M cut her short.

"Yes, Home Secretary, I'm well aware, I have the resignation letters on my desk."

She threw her bundle of folders across the desk where they skidded and toppled onto one of the many empty chairs.

"Some would say Capitalism at its best; I'd just say spineless money-grabbing bastards."

Most of the members of the British Cabinet had come to the conclusion that the situation was hopeless. Some had decided to retire and had taken up residence where they were now exiled. They could easily live off their savings that were safely invested in offshore accounts. A significant number had taken up job offers with foreign companies where their expertise and the fact that they were mates with the CEOs of multi nationals would ensure them a lucrative income and a lifestyle befitting their inflated egos.

"Well we'd best soldier on. Have you got anything like a report to give, Home Secretary?"

"Not a lot has changed since the last time we met. MI6 has reported that there are still several pockets of resistance operating, and in particular the lone operator has checked in using short coded messages on a restricted frequency. They haven't been able to establish where he is but he's still operational."

The Prime Minister finally sat down. "What about you, Foreign Secretary?"

"We still can't get any solid offers of help; foreign governments are becoming more evasive by the day."

"Have we had anything from the Americans?"

"Not a thing, but I have been told by a reliable source that they are entering into trade talks with the two new British Governments."

The silence in the room was palpable as the PM just stared at the last speaker. Getting up from her chair, she made her way towards the door. The Foreign Secretary cleared his throat.

"I'm leaving for Brussels in the morning Prime Minister; I've been offered a job with the European Commission."

QUATFORD

The village of Quatford, like many of the villages all around the country, looked deserted - but that didn't mean that David and Alice were going to be any less vigilant. Their progress down the small lane towards the river was slow. They stuck to the road but it was edged on both sides by dry stone walls for the most part which left very little room to dive into a hiding place if needed.

There was a busier minor road to cross as well before they could gain access to the river. Fortunately, the road did not seem to be getting any use, and they quickly dashed across, to find a sizeable drop on the other side. Jumping down, they were now out of sight of any road traffic.

From that point on, it was just a matter of yards to the riverbank. Once there, the two of them looked upstream and down, but there was not a boat to be seen. David pointed to a house a few hundred yards upstream.

"That place there might have a small boat in the garage, it looks posh enough."

They set off and found, on arrival, that it did have a boat house. It was the work of a few moments to break in. Inside was a small cabin cruiser. David threw his gear into the back, jumped in, and held out his hand to help Alice.

"Well thank you, kind sir. Kindly start the engine and let's be on our way."

"I don't think that's a very good idea, we'd have every terrorist in the area after us. We'll just cast off and drift down the river looking like we've slipped our moorings."

Alice just stuck her tongue out at him. "All right know all. I wish you'd stop treating me like an idiot. Do I have to remind you that you wouldn't be here if I hadn't rescued you?"

Now it was David's turn to pull a face. "Surely you mean 'aye aye, captain'?"

The dog wasn't keen. He sat on his haunches, quivering, before finally making the jump onboard. As soon as he had, he ducked inside, and after circling half a dozen times, settled down in the bow on top of a pile of towels.

It was slow going on the river. There wasn't much of a current and they just drifted to the opposite bank, eventually coming to a stop under some overhanging trees.

David decided that he would have to rethink his plan. Using a tarpaulin that he found inside the cabin, he erected a rough shelter over the stern of the boat which just covered the steering wheel. He took care to leave part of it to trail in the water, making it look like the cover had just finished up there by accident.

Alice stayed in the cabin, and David lay in the back of the boat where he could see where they were going without himself being seen. When they again pushed off from the bank, he was able to steer them into the middle of the river and keep the boat there as they meandered downstream.

When it started to get dark again, they moored up at the first wooded area they could find, well away from any signs of life. After a hot meal, made with the last of the gas for the little camping stove, they settled down for a good night's sleep.

In the morning, at first light, they drifted off again, this time with Alice steering and David in the cabin. He had blocked out the side windows with some old curtains so that he couldn't be seen from the bank, leaving only a small forward-looking gap through which he could look out for trouble.

Travelling this way was almost idyllic; they kept conversation to a minimum and only in hushed voices as they were unsure how noise would travel over the water. David scrutinized each riverbank as best he could from his position, but could hardly detect any activity at all. At one point they

168

passed a riverside pub looking just as it would have done pre-war, from a distance, but as they got nearer they could see broken windows and doors put in. David found himself craving the old days, when a drink at a riverside pub on a warm summer's day would be heaven.

A few miles further downstream, David spotted what looked like a caravan site partially hidden behind some trees. He gestured to Alice to head for that bank, and she obliged. As the boat ground to a halt alongside a rickety old landing stage, she looked at him inquiringly and whispered "What's going on?"

David joined her in the rear of the boat and held on to the jetty with his hand whilst keeping under the tarpaulin.

"There's a caravan site just back there. I thought we might be able to stock up on some tinned food, and at the very least there might be some gas there. There's a pub as well so there's got to be something."

David tied up the boat just above the water line without showing himself, and they decided to wait till dusk to lessen the chances of being spotted.

The afternoon passed without incident until David felt a kick in the middle of his back. Alice hissed at him. "You're snoring; they can probably hear you in London."

He turned over and tried to go back to sleep, but he was wide awake now and, as the light was just beginning to fade, they decided it was time to take a closer look.

Taking handguns and an empty haversack to carry away any spoils, they crept out from under the cover one at a time, and stood on the jetty, looking furtively around them. The dog bounded off the boat and ran up the road, happy to be off the water and able to explore and stretch his legs.

The caravan site was two fields back from a single track road that led to a village. The entrance to the site was a little way up the track, and so they set out towards it, sticking as close to the hedge as was physically possible. The sign at the entrance read 'The White Hart Inn Caravan and Camping Park'.

Cautiously, they moved on. It was rare now to come across anyone in the countryside. Most residents of towns and villages who had survived the hostilities had been rounded up and moved into camps. Most of the conquering force that wasn't actively out searching for runaways kept to the towns and the few cities that hadn't been totally destroyed.

Where they were now was a case in point. There was probably not a living soul within a mile, but they had to treat every move like they were being watched.

The pub in its heyday would have been the sort of place where David would have been happy to stay on a bright summer's day in the garden or a cold winter's day inside in front of a roaring log fire. Now it was in a sorry state - walls pockmarked with bullet holes, and all the doors and windows smashed.

Alice pushed open the door, but then stepped back. It looked like all the locals had gathered there either to support each other or just to enjoy a last civilized drink. The floor was littered with bodies, people shot down where they had stood, defenceless; the bars and tables were covered with unfinished drinks.

Alice and David retreated and made their way to the rear of the building, entering through the kitchen. The electric had been cut off long ago, and any frozen or perishable goods had rotted; tinned goods were in large, unwieldy containers, so David liberated a bottle of scotch from the store cupboard and they left to explore the caravan site.

The approach from the road was eerily quiet and it was easy to see why. Someone had clearly ransacked the static caravans, and the site was deserted. Pitched tents had been torn open.

David headed for the caravans whilst pointing towards the tented area. "You search the tents, Alice, see if you can find any camping gas cylinders in particular. I'll go through the vans, try and find some food. Don't take too long, it's gonna be dark in 15 minutes."

The first van that he went into showed little sign of damage. There are few places to hide in a caravan, and it looked like everyone from the site was in the pub at the time the terrorists had arrived. Cupboard doors were smashed where someone had been searching, but their interest was obviously not food as they'd left the few cans that were there untouched.

David put the cans into his bag and moved onto the next. There were bullet holes in the door and its glass panel was smashed. Cautiously he went inside, but the pungent smell of death soon assailed his nostrils. At the far end lay an elderly gentleman with several bullet holes in his chest, his skin blackened by decomposition. A rat had eaten part of his shoeless foot. There were plenty of other sources of food for rats in the pub, they wouldn't go hungry for some time.

David found a couple of packets of pasta and a plastic container containing rice, and he couldn't help thinking that the old boy's healthy eating habits had done him no good at all.

There was just enough time to check out another unit before it got too dark to see, and he struck gold. Alice was going to be thrilled at the dozen Pot Noodles he found.

Alice and David arrived at the park entrance at the same time, and Alice looked wide eyed at David's bulging haversack. "Looks like you did all right. I've managed to find a couple of canisters of gas, should keep us going for a week."

"That's good cos you can overdose on Pot Noodles now. Shit, we don't have any water."

David handed his bag to Alice. "I reckon I saw some in the kitchen at the pub, a load of six packs piled against the fridge. You go back to the boat and I'll meet you there."

There were indeed a load of six packs there. David carried one in each hand by pushing his fingers through the plastic wrapper, and made his way back to the boat.

He heard the men before he saw them. They were shouting loudly at Alice as they wrestled to tie her hands behind her back. One of them was more interested in ripping her blouse open than securing her. Alice, never one to hide her charms, was happy to distract him by struggling just enough.

David realized that they were not going to get out of this situation quietly, and took drastic action. As he walked forward, he dropped the water bottles and took his pistol from his waist band. He shot the nearest man in the back of the head. Alice's face was splattered with the blood.

David couldn't believe how loud the noise was - the stillness of the night made it sound like a bomb exploding. The noise and the shock completely stunned the other man who turned towards David open mouthed and received the full force of the butt of David's handgun on his left temple. "Where the hell did they come from, Alice?"

"They jumped out from the trees when I got back to the boat."

There were a couple of cars parked near the jetty. Covered in leaves and dust, they had obviously been there since before the massacre in the pub. David tried the door of the nearest one and pulled it wide open. "We'll stick them in here and push the car in the river; it's pretty deep here, it should go under; we don't want them floating downstream."

They managed to bundle the man with half his head missing into the passenger seat, and Alice opened up the boot. "I think this other one's still alive. We don't want the bastard waking up while he's drowning."

David was starting to worry about Alice's homicidal attitude, but she had a point. He helped her to lift him in, and shut the boot. He let off the handbrake, and with very little effort they got the car moving; it slid almost silently into the water and submerged with very little fuss. David headed back and retrieved the dropped bottles of water.

"Right, we better get out of here; someone must have heard that shot, they could be here any minute."

"What about the dog? He hasn't come back."

David could see that she was upset, but there was little that they could do. "I'm sure he'll be all right, he can look after himself."

They both got under the tarpaulin at the rear of the boat, and David untied the rope holding it to the jetty. The plan was to get the boat to drift over to the opposite bank whilst getting some distance downstream, but the flow of the river was very gentle at this point, and the operation took some time.

Total darkness made manoeuvring dangerous, and at one point they ran aground mid-stream on a small sand bank. It seemed to take an age for the boat to rotate 180 degrees to free itself, but any attempt by David or Alice to help it along would be spotted by anyone on the bank.

After nearly an hour David was alarmed to realise that he could still see the jetty where they had landed, but was reassured that there had been no activity as yet in response to the gun shot.

They began to feel a lot safer when they rounded a bend in the river, and the drifting boat picked up speed. A brief break in the clouds allowed enough moonlight through to pick out overhanging trees beside the bank a short distance in front. Having managed to steer for that point, they spent the rest of the night concealed under the trees.

David was aware that they would have to abandon the boat before they got to Worcester, but he struggled to remember what other populated places they had to go through before they got there. He was pretty sure that Bewdley and Stourport were both on the route, but whether the river passed through the towns was something he just didn't know.

The whole trip could probably be made in a day just drifting, but what he really needed was a map - and he had left his at Winston's house when he left in a temper. He cursed the fact that people had become so reliant on smart phones for everything.

At first light they cast off, and slowly emerged from their hiding place before restarting the leisurely drift down river. Before long they were approaching a footbridge running from one side of the river to the other. David decided to pull into the bank, and got out to explore.

The road on the bank where they landed led to a car park. There would definitely not be any passing traffic up this dead end. They walked up a slight incline away from the river, and passed a small pub that someone had ambitiously named the Harbour Inn. David couldn't help wondering how on earth it had managed to stay open before the war given its location, and a look through its windows confirmed that it was devoid of life.

From outside the pub he could see further up the road a little humpback bridge, so he knew he was on the right track. In a matter of yards, he had found what he was looking for. Alice regarded him with more than a little puzzlement. "Arley Station. What's the good of a railway station, there's not going to be any trains?"

David continued towards the platform. "If I'm not mistaken this is a Severn Valley railway station and it's bound to have… yes, here it is."

He stopped in front of a large map in a glass cabinet fixed to the wall. Alice stabbed her finger at the little red arrow that proclaimed 'you are here'. "Well at least we know where we are now."

David took a pen knife out of his pocket and began to prize the cabinet open. The glass cracked as the frame buckled.

"It's a comprehensive map of the area showing the river as well as the railway tracks. It has all the bridges on it for as far as we're going."

He eased the map through a gap in the case and folded it up into a manageable size.

The walk back down from Arley Station was as uneventful as the walk up, but nevertheless they kept a vigilant eye out for any human activity, and saw none.

They resumed their drift down the river while David studied the newly acquired map. He could see that their immediate problem would be the three bridges to negotiate in relatively built-up areas - two near Bewdley and one in Stourport. The river would be wider at these points, so he figured that if they were negotiated in the dark they should be able to get away with it. They wouldn't be able to go much further until they had to moor up and wait for darkness, but at least they knew where they were now.

Alice was doing the undercover steering, and so he settled down to study the map some more. What he heard next sent a shiver down his spine.

The boat had obviously changed direction - as Alice steered it around a 90 degree bend in the river, suddenly there was the loud sound of rushing water.

David leapt to the front of the boat to look through the forward-looking gap in his window covering, and saw directly ahead large rocks that had been placed in the river to form artificial rapids. The boat was picking up speed towards them. There was a rock-free passage close to the bank, which hopefully would be wide enough and deep enough to accommodate the boat.

"Alice, over to the left, steer left!"

Alice pulled the steering hard over but unfortunately the boat started to go sideways on. She pulled the other way to straighten, and as the water carried it along it forced the boat through the gap with an alarming scraping noise. As they slowed, David inspected the hull for leaks. Finding none, he breathed a sigh of relief and settled back down again.

"Well done Alice, I never doubted you for a minute."

They selected an area of the bank further downstream where the boat would be well hidden, but they would still able to get on shore.

Alice went first, and came back after about five minutes.

"There's just a few holiday homes, cabins mostly, in woodland. We could break into one and knock up a decent meal while we wait for it to get dark."

"Okay, that sounds like a plan."

The two of them walked into the woods, and when they came to a clearing they selected one of the four chalets around the perimeter. Slowly, gently, removing one of the glass panels in the door, they managed to break in without making a sound. There was probably no one else around for miles, but there was no point in taking unnecessary risks.

Inside was a fully functioning kitchen with a Calor Gas stove and some tinned food. There was no water supply, so they reluctantly had to use some of their own meagre stock, but they soon settled down to a welcome meal, after which they dozed off.

Alice woke first, but left David to sleep while they waited for it to get dark. She tidied the place up on the off chance that the world would return to normal one day, and the owners would come back.

As soon as the light began to fade, they returned to boat, aware that they could get lost once complete darkness fell. They settled down in the boat and waited until it was safe to set off. David elected to do the steering for the first part. As they pushed off, he found himself praying that they wouldn't fail after having come this far.

There were signs of a built-up area long before they arrived at the first bridge. Luckily the sky had clouded over and the boat was just a dark shadow drifting down the river. David kept the boat mid-stream, and the river began to widen, helping them to avoid drawing attention.

The bridge was an old stone, three arch road bridge with very little traffic passing over it. The town itself was well populated, but the riverbank promenade that would have been teeming with people a year ago was now deserted.

Shortly after passing under the bridge they began to gather speed. David suspected they might be heading towards some sort of weir, but a weir was just a shallow stretch of river where the water moved considerably faster.

He swapped places with Alice later. Trying to guide the boat in little to no light was a strain on the eyes, and a fresh pair was just what was needed. The river was relatively straight for this section and the next bridge turned out to be much less of a problem than they expected. It was a modern, high, main road bridge which had fast moving traffic on it. However, anyone in a car would be unable to see anything on the river in the fleeting moment it took to cross.

The next part of the journey was uneventful until the lights of Stourport started to illuminate the night sky. This last bridge had the potential to be the most dangerous, positioned as it was near the centre of the town. Alice was back doing the steering.

It had been over an hour since going under the last bridge. As they approached, she could see that a river cruiser had partially sunk diagonally across the river just the other side of the bridge. It was impossible to pass through without colliding with it – so she steered to hit it almost head on. This caused their boat to rotate and slip through the gap between the bow of the cruiser and the far bank stern first.

They continued out through the town with the boat facing the wrong way. Nobody noticed.

As soon as they were safely away from any buildings, they found a place to tie up. The stress and eyestrain had begun to take a toll on both of them, and David broke open the bottle of Scotch. They tried to relax until dawn.

When they set off in the half-light it became more noticeable that there were many more mooring points and a lot more boats of differing shapes and sizes. Most boats were damaged in some way, some completely sunken whilst still tied up. Their own boat was not likely to raise an alarm drifting down stream - to all intents and purposes, just another boat to have come adrift.

David had just started to relax when he heard a loud crack from the direction of the riverbank, and a bullet hole appeared in the hull just behind his shoulder.

Another shot followed, causing a splash, and then another holed the boat just below the water line. Through the hole created by the first bullet David could see two bearded men sitting at a table in the car park of a riverside pub. Both had rifles and had decided to pass the time of day with some target practice. He hurriedly plugged the hole in the floor with an old rag and turned to check on Alice. She was pressing herself hard to the floor of the boat, making no attempt at steering.

The two men were obviously lousy shots - as the angle between them and the boat grew, they found it increasingly difficult to find their mark. Both boat and occupants managed to survive without any serious damage or injury.

Some two hours later the boat drifted under yet another road bridge completely unnoticed, but their waterway journey came to an end when they came across a lock that they couldn't negotiate.

Sitting patiently on the riverbank was the dog. He had made the journey on foot rather than suffer the boat trip. Alice was so pleased to see him that she fed him half a packet of biscuits. Back in the house where they first found the dog or rather he found them, they saw he had a collar but no name tag. They tried calling him a few different names but got no response so they just called him 'dog' and he seemed to respond to that.

They abandoned the boat and prepared for the long hike overland. David had calculated that they were just outside Worcester, and according to the old boy they had met a few days before on the canal, they only needed to make it across to the river Avon and they would be safe.

RUTH & RALPH

It would have been easy to settle for the life in the bunker. It was safe and warm, and there were plenty of things to do. After a week or so, relationships were beginning to form.

Ralph had talked to Ruth at length about moving on, and she had agreed that she wouldn't find anywhere better if she got to where she wanted to be. The difference would be the chance that David might be there, or on his way.

There was a lot of countryside between where she was and her destination, and Ruth realized that a trip that would take a day walking on roads would take two or three over land.

Once she had made it clear that she was going to move on, the main concern was how she would protect herself. The weapons her group had arrived with would be needed by those remaining in the bunker, but she was reluctant to travel completely unarmed. Ralph solved the problem, announcing that he would go with her, and return with the weapons.

Ralph and Ruth left the estate after a prolonged round of emotional goodbyes at around midday. Tommo had declared that he was going to be in the area tracking troop movements for at least the first day that they were on their route.

Ruth had a slight twinge of regret as it started to rain, but they were equipped with gear to keep them dry, and at least there would be fewer of the occupying forces out and about in bad weather.

The track across the estate was relatively exposed, and they did have to dive for cover when a helicopter was in the area – but as they could hear it coming from a long way off, they were well hidden as it passed overhead.

Ralph had studied the available maps in detail before they set out on their journey and had the preferred route, along with any diversions that they might need to take, committed to memory. They only needed to cross one 'A' road and the rest of the journey could be made over fields and along minor and single track roads.

There was no traffic at all on that 'A' road, and they managed to cross it without incident; but when they were just a field away, they had been surprised to hear what turned out to be a convoy of trucks heading off the main road and up a side road at speed.

Continuing on their journey, they eventually came upon a place where the convoy had stopped.

It was parked along the edge of a field, and a cold shiver ran down Ruth's back when she saw that the field had been partially excavated. The digger was still busy extending a very deep hole. Ruth and Ralph hid themselves where they were out of sight but could observe what was happening.

Several heavily armed men stood around the trucks, smoking and chatting away. Ruth's fears were realized as the canvas back of one of the lorries was momentarily pulled back, and she could see men packed inside, standing with their hands tied behind their backs. Ralph moved close to her and whispered in her ear: "Are you thinking what I'm thinking?"

Ruth nodded with a look of fear and loathing etched across her face. "Looks to me like there's going to be a massacre sometime soon."

Ralph started to walk away, but she grabbed him by the sleeve. "Where are you going? We can't just leave them."

"Ruth, there's nothing we can do. There must be at least 20 of them, the two of us can't take them on."

She pulled him down to the ground beside her. "We're not just walking away, we can't. There's got to be 150 hostages in the trucks. If we can release them they can easily overpower the guards."

Ralph asked her to consider if throwing away her life on a futile act was going to help anyone. Tears of frustration streamed down her face. "Where's Tommo when you need him?"

*   *   *

Tommo was, in fact, exactly where you would need him in a situation such as this - less than half a mile away on top of a church tower with unrestricted views of the situation unfolding in front of Ralph and Ruth. His main problem was that he had broken a golden rule and not left himself an easy exit. Even with the abseil rope he'd left down the side of the church he was in grave danger of being trapped up there.

He had counted nineteen hostiles including the digger driver, and he knew that the odds were against him getting more than half. The hostages might help if any of them got free but that was unlikely. He needed an edge to give him an upper hand. It came as no surprise to realise that Ruth was going to provide that edge.

Ruth was stealthily making her way around the field to where the trucks were parked. The guards had started to unload the hostages from the trucks and were shoving them forward towards the trench. Tommo was trying to keep one eye on Ruth and the other on the execution squad.

The trucks nearest to Ruth were now empty of captives. She reached the first truck and unscrewed the cap on the fuel tank; then she seemed to sniff it and move on to the next truck. This next one was obviously petrol, so Tommo surmised that the first must have been diesel. She pushed a rag into the tank, lit it using the cigarette lighter she had brought for lighting the cooking stove, and quickly dived back to the other side of the hedge.

Tommo realized there would be a delay before anything happened, and turned his attention back to the hostages. A guard was forcing the first six onto their knees; suddenly the guard too fell to his knees, and tumbled into the trench.

The crack from Tommo's gun couldn't be heard from the field, and he despatched three more guards before anyone realized what was going on. Just at that moment, the truck blew up, lifting well off the ground. The guards began to panic, and the hostages started to run in all directions.

Instead of trying to locate and engage whoever was firing at them, the guards began indiscriminately shooting at the fleeing hostages. Ralph and Ruth stepped into the field from opposite sides and began trying to pick off the guards. Tommo carried on taking out as many as possible.

Three uniformed men stepped into the field from a wooded area at the back of the killing field, and began shooting at the guards too - and suddenly, it was all over. The three remaining guards gave up and surrendered, and all the hostages who were still alive had scattered and disappeared.

Everything happened so quickly that Ruth couldn't process most of it. The thing that was etched on her mind was the sight of the guards killing the unarmed prisoners, and she struggled to control her temper. She was on the verge of screaming, when one of the newcomers spoke to her. "You okay, Mam?"

She jumped with fright; she was aware of people joining in the fight against the guards, but she hadn't thought about who they were. These three were kitted out the same as Tommo. He had hinted but never confirmed that he was SAS, but the way these men had conducted themselves made her pretty sure that they were, too.

Asked about why they were here and where they had come from, Ruth was answering their questions when Tommo arrived. Greetings were exchanged and the four soldiers went off into a huddle.

Ralph was standing over the three guards, who he had made kneel on the ground near the pit, when the soldiers came back over to him and Ruth.

"Right, we all need to get out of here as soon as possible. We made a lot of noise, although they must have been expecting to make a lot of noise themselves. That truck explosion might arouse some curiosity."

Tommo went to shake hands with Ralph and Ruth. "These lads are going to come back to Blenheim with me; it should be a good base for us to work from. I assume you and Ruth are going to press on to the safe zone. I suggest we tie these three guards up and hope they don't get found too soon. It's a pity we can't shoot them, but they're prisoners of war, after all, and we're soldiers."

Ruth, still seething from what she had seen the guards do, took Tommo's pistol from its holster. "Yeah, but I'm not."

She shot each one in the back of the head and they fell into the trench. Then she handed the pistol back to a stunned Tommo.

Ruth and Ralph made a quick exit and were already a couple of fields away when the other trucks started to blow up. The SAS guys were not worried about attracting attention – they, too, had already disappeared into the countryside.

Concerned to put as much distance between them and the scene of the executions, Ralph maintained a steady jog until Ruth had to ask him to stop. Ralph insisted that they keep moving even if it was only at a walking pace.

Ruth had begun to suffer from shock at what she had done; her hands started shaking uncontrollably. The incessant marching helped to take her mind off things, but it was useless trying to retrieve anything from her pockets or adjust the straps of the gear she was carrying. When they eventually stopped and made a camp in a small thicket, she quickly got into her sleeping bag to try to disguise her trembling legs and feet.

Ralph had noticed, but decided to say nothing, and eventually she feel into a fitful sleep.

When she awoke in the morning the shaking had stopped, but she felt as though she had the mother of all hangovers. Ralph was fixing up a brew on the small gas stove they had brought with them, and his breath steamed from his mouth as he spoke. "We can't be far away now; how are you feeling this morning?"

Ruth hadn't realized how cold it was until she pulled her hands from the depths of her sleeping bag. "Better than I did last night. I hope we make it today, I'm pretty bloody sick of this shit."

Ralph nodded in agreement. "We need to be extra careful today, we don't want to be caught now that we're this close."

They set off again for the neutral zone, and although they kept away from roads, Ruth did see road signs that pointed to villages with familiar names. Then, as they reached the brow of a hill, they could see the neutral zone in the distance.

Barbed wire fixed to wooden trusses six feet high stretched as far as the eye could see in both directions. Occasional craters on the other side of the fence showed where some unsuspecting animal had set off one of the mines laid in a continuous line along the fence.

Ralph tried to lighten the mood.

"We'll be okay. Steve McQueen will be along with his motorbike in a minute."

As they approached the fence across the last field, Ruth began to see that this was not going to be easy. It was conceivable that they could make some sort of ladder to facilitate getting on top of the structure, but it was a long drop the other side. There was no sign of life either way up or down the fence, just the endless barrier stretching for miles. They started to walk to the east hoping to find something different that would allow them to get across, and they must have covered over two miles when a voice from the other side of the fence hailed them. "You looking to get in the neutral zone?"

Startled, Ruth peered into the darkness of the thicket the other side. "Yes, we are, is there any way across?"

"Is it just the two of you?"

Ruth looked at Ralph and he shook his head.

"No it's just me, Ralph has to go back."

She unslung the AK47 from her shoulder and went to pass it to Ralph. The man in the woods interrupted her.

"You need to bring the gun, we need things like that."

Ruth hadn't expected this, she had to send the gun with Ralph, it was needed more at Blenheim. She started to feel a sense of panic, and then she remembered. "I have penicillin, and I'm a qualified nurse, surely that will be more useful than a gun?"

The voice from the woods became more authoritative and addressed Ralph.

"You need to go now before we show the lady how to get across."

Ruth gave her gun to Ralph and hugged him; she found it hard to let him go. "Thanks for everything Ralph, good luck with the rest of your life."

He walked away without looking back. A tear ran down his cheek and he wiped it away with his sleeve, blaming the wind for making his eyes water. When he was finally out of sight over the hill the voice from the woods told Ruth to continue walking in the same direction that she had been going. After about ten minutes walking a man suddenly appeared from a hole in the ground in front of her; it was the entrance to a covered tunnel. "I'm going to have to search you. I'm sorry, it's quite intrusive."

Ruth held up her arms for the search. He didn't make any allowances for her being a woman, and Ruth felt a little violated, but she had the impression that if she hadn't allowed it the man would have shot her. He relieved her of her pistol which he put into his jacket pocket.

"You can have that back the other side if everything checks out."

He pointed to the tunnel entrance. "It's dark down there but it is dry and bug free, comes up just past the tree line. After you."

Ruth scrambled down the tunnel followed by the man, who stopped only to replace the camouflaged cover behind him.

DAVID AND ALICE

According to his map, David could see that as they were still far enough north of Worcester, their only problem was going to be the M5 motorway. Worcester was densely populated by the northern denominations of the rebel forces that had divided the country, but the town seemed to be serviced by the roads leading into it from the north. That left the road David and Alice were walking parallel to almost deserted. In fact, the western end of that road - unknown to them - had been closed off for reasons that became apparent as they approached the rugby football stadium next to the motorway.

The stench of rotting flesh was noticeable more than a mile from the stadium, and by the time they reached the car park it was bad enough for David to realize that there was nothing to be gained from going inside. He couldn't even hazard a guess at how many unfortunate souls had met their end in that enclosed space, but given the length of time that had passed since the start of the war, he could be pretty certain that there was no one living left inside.

The closure of the road did have an upside - in the half light of the evening they were able to cross the motorway without fear of being seen.

As soon as they were across, they left the road for the relative security of the fields. Progress was much slower, but with little chance of being seen, it was the better option. All the roads this side of the motorway were unused as they only led to the neutral area.

It was now just a matter of walking until they reached the outskirts of Stratford, but as darkness fell, they decided to bed down for the night and make the final journey early the next morning.

It was an incident-free night, and they continued onwards at dawn. It wasn't very long before they encountered the high wood and razor wire construction that was the barrier between the northern forces and the safe zone. The dog summed up the mood of the party as he sat on his haunches and stared, looking puzzled, at the fence.

As things turned out, the border fence here had been built down the middle of a minor road. The three of them began to walk east along the road while they looked for inspiration in how to get across.

Eventually they reached a terrace of three houses, built right up to the edge of the road. Instead of leaving a gap, the fence had been constructed right up to the houses.

David could see potential here. He began to look around for farm buildings on their side of the fence. Not too far up ahead he spotted what he was looking for, and while Alice and the dog settled themselves comfortably in a ditch out of sight, he set off alone for the farm.

Less than an hour later, Alice was startled by the approach of a vehicle, and made sure she and dog were well concealed until it passed. But it didn't pass; it came to a stop right in front of where she was hiding.

"Alice! Alice, it's only me."

She peered out from her hiding place to see David at the wheel of a tractor with a large front loader.

"What the hell are you going to do with that?"

David elevated the front bucket to its full height, and swung it over the fence till it smashed through the window of the house opposite. He swung it back and dropped it to the ground.

"You and dog get in and hold on."

After one false start, when dog jumped out, David managed to deposit Alice and dog through the window of the house in the neutral zone. Then, using the cabled remote on the tractor, he was able to get himself across and – for good measure - returned the front loader to its ground position.

The sense of freedom once on the other side was palpable. They walked almost without caution actively seeking out roads rather than avoiding them. These were roads that David knew, roads that led home.

In no time at all they came across a farm, and the occupants, a middle aged man and his wife, invited them in, happy to feed them and even offer a bed for the night. Apparently refugees arriving in the safe zone were few and far between these days, as many people didn't believe that it existed. The couple reassured them that they no longer had anything to fear as they themselves had been there for four months with no sign of trouble. The two opposing sides of the conquering army were happier to use the buffer zone rather than sort out their differences with violence.

They politely declined the couple's hospitality, and, after enjoying sandwiches and freshly brewed tea, carried on their way. David had found a renewed sense of urgency about returning home and the possibility of finding Ruth there. They passed a few houses along the road towards Stratford, and people who saw them coming came out to greet them.

David was torn between his desire to get home as soon as possible, and the forgotten pleasure of passing the time of day with friendly folk. But eventually they reached the top of his road, and there ahead of him was home.

The cherry tree in the front garden was in full bloom, a mass of pink obscuring the house. It looked almost the same as when he had left it, and his pulse began to race at the thought of Ruth being there.

As they drew nearer it became obvious that the house was empty. Cobwebs covered the windows, and a mass of rubbish and leaves had piled against the bottom of the door, blown there by the wind.

He led Alice to the back of the house and found the spare key in its hiding place in the shed. Once inside, the emptiness was evident everywhere: dust was on every surface, cobwebs in all the corners, and it had the general damp smell of a place that no one had used for some time.

David cursed himself for thinking that Ruth would arrive before him; he had no idea of what hardships she might have had to suffer. Alice got busy airing some bedding she had found in a cupboard, while David cleaned up two of the three bedrooms as best he could. A good stress-free night's sleep was what they both needed.

Over the next few days, Alice and David set about restoring the house to its former glory. David sorted out his old pushbike, and made the short trip to the outskirts of town where he was surprised to find the supermarket open. There were two armed guards at the door.

"Don't look so worried mate; we're only here to ensure fair play. Are you new to the neutral zone?"

David nodded his head, somewhat taken aback by the friendliness coming from heavily armed men. "Yes, me and my, errr, friend, we got here a couple of days ago."

"Okay just register with the guy inside; he'll tell you what's what."

David went inside to find an elderly man sitting behind a desk, who explained that they had formed a sort of survivor's co-operative. They were using the non-perishable supplies in the shop to supplement co-op members until they had the chance to get their own smallholdings up and running, and could grow their own food.

"Don't take more than you need; when it's gone we can't get more. The shelves are labelled with the ration amounts. There's a seed and seed potato section at the back of the shop if you want to get started on your growing."

David filled a couple of carrier bags with all he could carry on the bike. As he left, he asked the friendly guards: "How many people are in this area then?"

"There's 37 registered to this shop. The other supermarkets have their own co-ops. We take it in turns to guard, if you fancy a go."

David called back over his shoulder, as he wheeled his heavily-laden bike across the car park,

"Sure, I don't mind taking a turn."

David and Alice busied themselves planting out the greenhouse and the garden, and the garden of the empty house next door. Days began to turn into weeks, and although David was very grateful for his friendship with Alice, he struggled to stop their relationship turning into something else.

Alice had begun to take trips into town, and David found himself wishing that she would strike up a relationship with someone else.

During the day the two of them worked on the gardens, and in the evenings Alice would settle down in the house with a book and some wine from David's considerable wine collection.

On warm evenings, David would sit in the front garden under the cherry tree, with dog resting his head on his feet, keeping watch in the hazy evening light for any sign of Ruth.

Summer slowly began to fade into early autumn, but the weather stayed warm, and David continued his evening vigil, sitting in his old garden chair. One evening, as often happened, the warmth of the evening sun and the hypnotising sound of insects soon had him dozing off, and he would once again dream of Ruth.

Lying back in the chair, eyes shut and face titled to the setting sun, he felt the dog stir, and begin the rumblings of a low growl. Reluctantly, David began to drag himself out of his reverie and back to consciousness. "What's the matter, Dog" he asked, stretching his left arm out to pat the dog. "What's bothering you?"

Slowly he opened his eyes, blinking into the evening sun. Covering his eyes with his right hand, he tried to see what dog had spotted. As he stared ahead, a shimmering figure came into view. If it hadn't been for dog, he would have thought he was still dreaming. But the figure grew nearer, waved, and finally broke into a run. David could doubt himself no longer, as he heard that oh so familiar and long-awaited voice call out: "David!"

The Girl from Whitfield Hall

Pete Harrison

Emily, a girl from a wealthy family, struggles to find her place in the London of the Great War. Driven by a desire to succeed in a man's world she reinvents herself as a male detective in the capital's Police Force. When her brother is accused of killing a girl in France, she goes to his aid.

Available in paperback, Kindle and Audible.